MURDER IN THE HIGHLANDS

DEBBIE YOUNG

Boldwood

First published in Great Britain in 2023 by Boldwood Books Ltd.

Copyright © Debbie Young, 2023

Cover Design by Head Design Ltd

Cover Photography: Shutterstock

A CIP catalogue record for this book is available from the British Library.

Paperback ISBN 978-1-80483-127-4

Large Print ISBN 978-1-80483-126-7

Hardback ISBN 978-1-80483-128-1

Ebook ISBN 978-1-80483-125-0

Kindle ISBN 978-1-80483-124-3

Audio CD ISBN 978-1-80483-134-2

MP3 CD ISBN 978-1-80483-132-8

Digital audio download ISBN 978-1-80483-130-4

Boldwood Books Ltd
23 Bowerdean Street
London SW6 3TN
www.boldwoodbooks.com

Bjorn Larsson, this one's for you
With much love from Sophie and Hector

In the afternoon, a customer spent an hour wandering around the shop. He finally came to the counter and said, 'I never buy second-hand books. You don't know who else has touched them, or where they've been.'

— SHAUN BYTHELL, PROPRIETOR OF THE BOOKSHOP IN WIGTOWN, IN *THE DIARY OF A BOOKSELLER*

1

ON THE WRONG TRACK

'Don't do it, Sophie!' cried Carol, clasping her hands as if in prayer.

I set a bar of chocolate on the shop counter and reached into my handbag for my purse.

'But it's the smallest one in the shop,' I protested, handing her a £1 coin. 'And I'll share it with Hector when I get to work. Whatever's left of it by then, anyway.'

Lately I'd got into the bad habit of treating myself each morning to some chocolate from the village shop on my way to Hector's House, the bookshop where I ran the tearoom. Carol's admonishing remark pricked my conscience.

'I'm not talking about the chocolate, you daftie.' She scanned the barcode on the chocolate wrapper and pressed the button to open the till. After dropping my coin into the cash drawer, she pressed my change into my open palm, and when I curled my fingers over it, she wrapped both her hands around mine and held them there.

'I mean your elopement,' she continued. 'Running away with Hector to get married is a great mistake. You'll hurt your parents, your friends, and your neighbours, and you'll find out all too late that you've hurt yourself too. Take my advice, give that Greta Garbo a miss.'

She meant Gretna Green, of course, the historic village just north of the border, famous as the wedding destination of eloping couples. There was the tinkle of broken glass from the stockroom at the back of the shop, where Carol's new boyfriend Ted was unpacking the day's deliveries from their wholesaler. Theirs was a mid-life romance, and they'd been dating only since Valentine's Day.

Carol glanced down the aisle in his direction. 'You okay, love?'

An affirmative grunt was his reply, followed by the sound of footsteps on the stairs to the flat above the shop. He'd either gone to find a plaster for the damage he'd done to himself with whatever he'd broken or to make himself a restorative cup of tea. Ted was a sturdy chap, in his fifties – like Carol – and clumsy. His presence as a part-time voluntary shop assistant was possibly a mixed blessing, but he did supply excellent fresh bread every day from his home-based bakery.

Before I could respond to Carol's advice, the Reverend Murray, who had been lingering by the R to S shelves deliberating between Rich Tea biscuits and shortbread, came to join us, a packet of each in his hands.

'Good morning, Sophie.' His expression was unusually serious. 'I must say I'm disappointed to hear you prefer a civil ceremony to a church wedding, especially when you have our beautiful parish church of St Bride's at your disposal, with all your friends and neighbours nearby.' He set the biscuits down on the counter. 'Would you be so kind as to put these on my account, please, Carol?'

Carol pulled the old-fashioned ledger out from under the

counter and flipped it open at the M section. The vicar must have known that Carol's disastrous elopement when she was a young woman had coloured her advice to me. But her situation then was entirely different from mine now. I'd been in a stable relationship with Hector for a year, whereas hers had been a rash, unguarded decision to run away with a man she barely knew.

Besides which, I had no intention of getting married for a very long time, not even to Hector. After all, I was only twenty-six. I was in no rush, and nor was he.

'Why is everyone convinced Hector and I are eloping to Gretna Green?' I tried not to sound as cross as I felt. 'All we're doing is taking a short holiday in Scotland to visit my parents. He's never spent any time with them. Their only previous encounter was at Great-auntie May's funeral.'

Carol shook her head mournfully.

'Ah, dear old May Sayers.' May had been a good friend to Carol and her parents, especially during her mother's final, protracted illness. 'That's another reason you should have your wedding in the village. You'd be able to leave your bouquet on May's grave at the end of the day. I'd leave mine on my parents' grave if anyone ever asked me to marry them.' She gazed wistfully towards the stockroom.

'Not forgetting the colour and joy that our choir and bell ringers can add to your special day,' added the vicar, ever loyal to anyone who took part in the communal life of the church. 'And, after all, what better place can there be for a wedding than a church called St Bride's? I wonder which hymns you would choose for yours?'

I began to consider which would best suit the voices of our village choir, whose strongest attribute was their willingness. Then I clapped my hand to my face to bring myself to my senses, astonished at how easily these two village stalwarts were leading me astray.

'Listen, we're really not planning on getting married,' I declared. 'Either here or at Gretna Green, or anywhere else along the way.' I slipped my bar of chocolate into my pocket. 'We're just visiting my parents. I've hardly seen my parents since I moved to Wendlebury. It's high time they got to know Hector, and for him to get to know them too.'

Carol finished recording the vicar's brace of biscuit packets, closed the accounts book, and replaced it on its shelf below the counter. As she returned her attention to me, she brightened.

'Ah, I see. You're going to get your parents' approval before you get married.' She smiled as she scanned the barcodes on the vicar's biscuits to remove them from stock. 'Call me old-fashioned, but I think that's an excellent idea. I only wish—'

She stopped short of elaborating on her own experience. The vicar chipped in to spare her embarrassment.

'Who wouldn't approve of their daughter marrying a decent, honest, hard-working type like Hector Munro?' He beamed. 'And vice versa, my dear. Your match would certainly have my blessing.

I bit my lip.

'I appreciate your endorsement, Vicar, but it's just a holiday. Hector's not had a proper break all year, and he's never been to Scotland. But we're heading for Inverness, not Gretna Green.'

I chose not to reveal that we'd pass very close to Gretna on the way, keen to curtail the ever-active village rumour mill before things got completely out of hand.

After bidding them both goodbye, I left the shop and headed up the High Street to the bookshop, too distracted to remember the chocolate in my pocket until I was almost there.

The pair's comments had made me realise there was another

subconscious reason for our trip to Scotland that I hadn't acknowledged even to myself. I wanted Hector to understand my affection for Inverness and the Highlands, where I'd spent my formative teenage years, and for him and my parents to get to know each other. But I also needed to reassure myself that, away from our mutual comfort zone, Hector was a keeper.

2

SECOND BEST

'Who's Maggie Burton?' I asked Hector, as we sat in the tearoom
during a quiet spell later that morning, deliberating over
applications for temporary staff to run Hector's House while we
were away. I held up a hand-written letter on mauve deckle-
edged notepaper. It was an old-fashioned brand my Auntie May
had favoured for correspondence when she wasn't abroad on
her travel-writing expeditions. Most of my letters from her had
been penned on crisp, fine, pale-blue airletter stationery, and
boasted a fine array of picturesque stamps from around the
world. I'd kept them all.

Hector groaned, covering his face with his hands. 'Oh,
please, not Maggie Burton!' He peeked at me through his
fingers. 'You know, the lady who wanted the blue book.'

I poured us each another cup of tea. 'Oh yes, I remember!' I
grimaced in sympathy.

Maggie Burton was a relative newcomer to the village,
having recently moved into a sixties bungalow set back in an old
orchard just off the main road. She had made her first visit to the
shop during the week that I was away in Greece.

Her book requests had since become legendary at Hector's House for their obscurity, and Hector had been known to hide when he saw her coming, leaving me to decipher her descriptions. The latest request had been for a book by David Attenborough about interior design. It was blue and had a picture of a whale on the cover, she'd said confidently. After what felt like a round of the old parlour game of Twenty Questions, I'd realised it was the recent memoir by a marine wildlife documentary-maker which included anecdotes of filming David Attenborough's *Blue Planet* series. *The Whale in your Living Room* had been on display in our shop window for the last week. I'd fetched it for her only to have her say, 'You see, I told you it was blue!'

Then, as with all the books we found for her, she'd held it, sniffed it, glanced at the back cover without reading the blurb, and turned her watery grey eyes on me in appeal. 'But do you think I'll enjoy it?'

The thought of Maggie Burton manning the trade counter, even for the single week that Hector and I would be in Scotland, was too alarming for us to take her application seriously.

'Can you imagine? I can picture her asking every customer who comes to the trade counter to buy a book "But do you think you'll enjoy it?"'

'Ha!' Hector got up to fetch a cookie jar from the tearoom counter, unscrewing the lid on his way back to our table and offering me a chocolate biscuit before taking one himself.

'Perhaps I should create a new position for her: Sales Prevention Officer. Who else have we got?'

I picked up the other envelope, a plain white one addressed in careful block capitals, and slit it open with the knife beside my tea plate. Carefully I removed the sheet of paper it contained.

'Oh, it's from Ted!'

'Really? I thought he was fully employed, in between his baking and helping Carol?'

Ted's small but enthusiastic round of local retail deliveries took up the early part of his day, and Carol's shop the rest of it, not to mention the actual baking.

'We'd better not let him loose in the tearoom,' I said, remembering his accident in Carol's stockroom earlier. 'He'd wreck the place on his first day.'

I felt very protective of the tearoom. In the year since Hector had employed me, I'd been steadily building up the financial contribution it made to the bookshop, which needed every extra income stream we could think of to keep it in profit. Even though the business belonged entirely to Hector, I'd have hated Ted to undo my hard work. Hector took the letter from me and read it in silence.

'To be fair, he's got a lovely way with people, despite his shyness. I can see him holding the fort at the trade counter well enough. After all, you can't easily break a book or do any damage with one. Plus, he's physically fit and strong. He'd easily lift any heavy deliveries, and he's tall enough to reach the top shelves without a ladder.'

'Then I think the decision is a no-brainer, provided he can finish his bread deliveries before our opening time. Bakers usually start and finish early, don't they? Like milkmen. So, what happens next? Will you talk to him about it or do you want me to? I can nab him in the village shop on my way home if you like.'

Hector gave a wry grin.

'Yes, it's probably better if you handle the next stage of the recruitment process. You know my usual form from when I recruited you last year, Sophie.'

I had to smile.

'What, you mean get the candidate tiddly, then sleep with them a few months down the line?'

When I'd applied, Hector had been distilling hooch to slip into the tea of favourite customers, describing it as his 'special cream'. I was thankful I'd persuaded him to put a stop to that this summer before it landed him in trouble.

He reached across the table to take my hands and gave them a tender squeeze.

'Play your cards right, sweetheart, and you could be on course for a promotion.'

I pulled a hand free to cuff his head affectionately before starting to clear the paperwork away. As his only employee, I didn't see how promotion could be possible, even though Hector acknowledged the business had benefited from my marketing instincts and ideas. When I'd started working at Hector's House, the tearoom had just been a service to customers of the bookshop. I'd turned it into a destination in its own right. Yet after twelve months, I was still working the same hours and earning the same wages. Perhaps when we came back from Scotland, I should press him for a pay rise. I'd think about it.

'So, if Ted runs the bookshop while we're away, where does that leave the tearoom?' I tried to keep my voice neutral. 'Without the tearoom, he'll sell far fewer books.'

Hector blinked hard twice, as if rebooting his thought process.

'How about Mrs Wetherley?' She was the lady who provided our home-baked cakes, scones and biscuits. A recently retired food-technology teacher, she regarded her service to us as a way of financing what was now her hobby of baking. It also relieved her of the need to either eat all her produce herself or to hold enough tea parties and coffee mornings for friends and relations to eat it for her.

Hector frowned. 'I'm not sure she'd want to be in the shop nine till five. She might get bored and rather be baking.'

I bit back a retort about whether I might ever crave more action as I manned the tearoom all day.

'Maybe if you said she could bake on the premises, so she's not having to go home and bake in the evenings to replenish stock. That might even be an advantage, wafting delicious baking aromas around the shop, along with the scent of fresh coffee.'

Hector gazed at me for a moment before his face relaxed into a smile.

'That's an excellent idea, Sophie. I'm not sure there's room to make it work on a long-term basis, as there's not much room to move behind the counter, and the cooker is quite small, but she might make it work just for the week we're away. I'll phone her tonight and ask her. Well done.' He slapped his thighs. 'So that's all sorted then. Assuming Ted and Mrs Wetherley say yes, anyway.'

I tidied away our cups and returned the cookie jar to its usual place on the tearoom counter, feeling glum that I could be so easily replaced. What's more, Mrs Wetherley was a much better baker than me.

3

PACKING UP OUR TROUBLES

As I sat on Hector's bed, watching him fill his battered backpack for our departure the next morning, I realised I'd been putting off describing my parents for fear of, well, putting him off.

'Dad says Mum lost her spark after Suzy died.'

Hector was rolling seven pairs of socks into seven neat balls and stuffing them into the bottom of the backpack, eyes narrowed in concentration.

'Who's Suzy?'

I leaned back against the headboard, drew my knees up and looped my arms around them.

'Mum's best friend. Mum's late best friend. After growing up virtually in each other's pockets in their home village in Kent, and going through their entire school education together, they went to different universities and never lived close to each other again. But they stayed in touch, and every year or so, they'd get together at Suzy's or at ours and make up for lost time. They were quite different in lots of ways. Suzy was a scientific boffin type, while Mum studied languages. Suzy was a night owl, always wanting to be out after dark stargazing, while Mum's a lark, the sort who'd happily go for a run before breakfast or an early-morning dip, but be spark out by 9 p.m. Suzy couldn't have cared less about her looks, while Mum has always taken pride in her appearance.'

Hector pulled a couple of pairs of jeans from his wardrobe and laid them on the bed.

'Yes, I remember thinking at May's funeral that she was very attractive for her age.' He ducked to avoid the pillow I threw at him.

'But they got along because they respected each other's interests and indulged them. All very well until they went one step too far, about ten years ago, when I was still at school. Suzy, overzealous in embracing Mum's passion for swimming, managed to get herself drowned when she came up to visit Mum in Scotland and they went on trip to the Outer Hebrides together.'

Hector set down the pair of jeans he'd been rolling up and came to sit beside me, putting a comforting arm about my shoulders.

'How on earth did that happen? Don't they have lifeguards at Scottish swimming pools?'

I looked away. 'It wasn't at a swimming pool, not the indoor kind that you mean. They were outdoors, on a beautiful beach on the Isle of Harris. The sort with pearly white sand and turquoise seas, a vast, deserted beach backed by wild machair.'

'Wild what?'

'Machair. That's a sort of grassy dune area that marks where the beach meets the land. It's really pretty.'

Hector turned to kiss my temple.

'Sounds more like the Maldives. I had no idea they had beaches like that in Scotland.'

I rested my head on his shoulder.

'There's a lot you don't know about Scotland yet. Anyway, they'd gone to stay on Lewis and Harris for a couple of days. They're actually two halves of the same island. Suzy was enraptured by the clarity of the sky at night. No light pollution, you see. Mum fell asleep stargazing with Suzy, and the next thing she knew, Suzy was gone. She'd tried to take a moonlit dip while Mum was asleep, and, not knowing the area like Mum did, she'd been ignorant of the local tide patterns and had been swept out to sea and drowned. That beautiful sea may look innocuous, but strong currents and the cold can take you unaware and kill you in no time. They found Suzy's body the next day, washed up further along the beach.' My voice cracked with emotion. I cleared my throat. 'So, long story short, don't expect Mum to come with us if we want to go swimming. She hasn't swum since, not even indoors. Man-made swimming pools never appealed to her anyway. It's such a shame for her. Dad says she's like a born singer silenced.'

Hector put his other arm round me and drew me close to him.

'I'm glad we've been stocking that book on wild swimming tips this summer. You never know: if Suzy had read a book like that, perhaps she'd be here still.' He shuddered. 'To be honest, I've never understood the appeal of wild swimming. It's just common sense that it's dangerous. Why take avoidable risks?'

'When I was growing up, we just called it swimming. It was our thing. Mum and I would swim. You can't really understand until you've tried it. The raw freedom, the feeling of being a part of the stunning scenery, the thrilling tingle of the chilly water that makes you feel so alive... So, Mum and I swam while Dad did his hills.'

'Hills? What sort of hills? What did he do in the hills?'

Hector got to his feet to resume his packing, while I sat, cross-legged twiddling my hair.

'What do you mean, what hills? The Munros, of course.'

He gazed at me blankly.

'You know, all the Scottish mountains over three thousand feet high. So-called because they were first mapped by a certain Sir Hugh Munro. Dad's a Munro-bagger. Gotta climb them all. Honestly, Hector, how did you reach your age, with your name, without knowing about the Munros?'

I pulled one of the pillows out from under me and hugged it to my chest.

'Well, you know now. And you'll know even better, once Dad's taken you up one, if Mum lets him.'

Hector pushed his hands down inside the backpack to compact his clothes before starting to add books from the pile beside the bed.

'Why wouldn't she let him? We're both grown-ups.'

I hugged the pillow.

'Suzy's accident made her risk averse. I'm lucky she still lets me go swimming at indoor pools. Which in the Highlands are fabulous, by the way, and there's a pool in Inverness that even has a little outdoor pool shaped like a thistle, but it's not the same as proper outdoor swimming in the wild. You have packed your swimming trunks, haven't you?'

I couldn't remember seeing him put them in.

Hector paused in the middle of buckling up the top of the backpack.

'To be honest, I don't currently own any.'

He looked away.

'What? How do I even go out with you?'

Hector raised his hands in surrender. 'Okay, okay, I'll buy

some when we get there if you really want me to.' He ran one hand through his dark curls.

I decided to be merciful and move back into his comfort zone. 'Don't forget Mum's book, either.'

'That's all under control. I left it on the trade counter when we shut up shop tonight so that I'll remember to pick it up first thing in the morning, after I've given Ted and Mrs Wetherley their final briefing.'

'We,' I said quickly. 'After *we've* briefed them. I can show Mrs Wetherley what's what in the tearoom while you take care of Ted. We want to get away as soon as we can. It's a five-hundred-mile journey, you know.'

I wished I'd learned to drive so that we could take turns at the wheel, instead of him having to do all the work.

'Now there's a cue for a song,' said Hector, and I knew he'd be setting that one up to play on the shop's sound system at the first opportunity.

I was glad he'd acquired a great gift to take for my mum – a vintage book of Gaelic poetry that he'd bought at a car boot sale back in January when we were visiting his parents in the little Somerset seaside town of Clevedon. After all, for me this trip would be a homecoming. For Hector it was a venture into a strange land. I hadn't realised just how alien he might find it until we'd had this conversation. Perhaps the Gaelic book might serve as a talisman – the bookseller's equivalent of a St Christopher medallion to ensure safe passage and a trouble-free return.

4

A WENDLEBURY SEND-OFF

By Monday morning, my fears had inverted. Now I was more anxious that Hector might dislike my parents, rather than the other way around. Faced with the prospect of intolerable in-laws, he might call our relationship off. Lovely as he was, working for an ex-boyfriend would be awkward. Besides, I enjoyed my job, despite my growing misgivings about the pay and status, and I'd be upset to have to give it up because of relationship issues.

By the time the bookshop opened, I was anxious to be on our way. With an estimated nine-hour drive ahead of us, not including stops, I'd have preferred an earlier start, but I gave in to Hector's insistence on a final brief to Ted and Mrs Wetherley, despite them already having had a couple of hours' training.

I'd spent the night at my cottage, enjoying a little solitude before spending every minute of the next week in Hector's company. When I arrived at the shop to meet Hector, I was surprised to find Kate, Hector's godmother, who also lived in the village, behind the trade counter. She beamed when she saw me.

'Hector asked me to keep an eye on the workers while you're

away,' she said in a low voice, while Hector was showing Ted something in the stockroom. 'I'll just pop in first thing and last thing each day to troubleshoot, and now and again if I'm passing. So, no need to worry, Sophie. Just relax and enjoy your holiday. Look after him.'

I suspect Kate, as Hector's godmother, still thinks of him as a little boy.

I smiled indulgently. To be honest, knowing Kate was going to oversee both the shop and the tearoom was reassuring. She's very sensible, having served on just about every committee in the community, and is regarded around the village as a safe pair of hands.

'I think he can take care of himself, actually,' I replied. 'After all, he's bigger and stronger than I am. Well, a few inches taller and wider, anyway. But I'll do my best to bring him back in one piece, I promise you.'

In the end, I had to physically frogmarch Hector out of the shop, interrupting his lecture to an increasingly anxious Mrs Wetherley. She'd looked perfectly confident before he started on her.

'Come on, Hector, your shop will be fine.' I picked up my backpack and heaved it onto my shoulder. 'We're only a phone call away if they get stuck with anything.'

I thought it better not to mention the frequent mobile black spots in the Highlands.

Just as we were stowing our luggage in the back of the Land Rover, Tommy and his little sister Sina came racing up the High Street, almost bumping into us as they screeched to a halt. Tommy produced from his parka pocket a small glass jar containing a caramel-coloured liquid. Sina reached out a hand to hold it too, indicating it was a gift from them both.

'"Local honey from Wendlebury Barrow hives",' I read from the label.

'It's for your honeymoon,' Sina explained, sounding pleased with herself. 'To help you have a happy marry in Scotland.'

Hector and I exchanged glances. We'd thought we'd managed to quash the elopement rumour, but we didn't want to hurt the children's feelings.

Old Billy emerged from around the corner, where Hector parked his Land Rover. Tommy and Sina turned to grin at him conspiratorially.

'All done, kiddies.' Billy tapped a finger against the side of his nose. 'Now, I'll race you to the churchyard. Remember the pair of you said you'd help me weed it after you-know-what.'

He turned to Hector and me and raised his battered cap.

'Now off with the pair of you,' he said, giving Hector the hugest of winks. 'You don't want to be late for your own wedding. Don't do anything I wouldn't do, boy.' He returned his attention to me. 'And don't you let him get away with nothing. He'll be under your thumb once you've married him, even if he is technically your boss in his shop. *Bon voyage* to you both, or whatever they say in Scottish.'

Leaving Hector and I lost for words, he followed the giggling children up the High Street. Hector closed the back door of the Land Rover and we climbed aboard.

Only as we pulled out onto the High Street did we become aware of a dreadful metallic rattling and scraping sound. Fearing damage to his precious vehicle, Hector parked outside the shop, jumped down from the driver's seat, and darted to the rear of the Land Rover to check the course of the stomach-churning noise.

I heard a rip of cardboard and turned to see him holding up a large hand-painted sign bearing the words 'Just married' with

'Later today' in brackets underneath. I immediately guessed the metallic sound had come from a traditional string of tin cans that Billy, Tommy and Sina must have tied to the rear bumper.

Hector paused by my window to speak to me, and I wound it down. 'I'll just get the scissors,' he said levelly, and disappeared inside the shop.

A moment later, he returned holding up the Gaelic book to show me.

'Maybe we should be thankful after all. If it hadn't been for those scallywags, we'd have driven off leaving your mum's book on the trade counter.'

Kate followed, scissors in hand. She swiftly cut off the strings of tin cans while Hector slipped the book into his pocket and climbed back into the driving seat.

'Now, for goodness' sake, you two, just go!' She waved, the scissors in one hand and the string of old cans dangling from the other. At last, we were on our way.

5

AN URGENT CALL

As soon as we'd passed the 'You're leaving Wendlebury Barrow' sign, on which some wag had graffitied, 'BUT WHY?', I began to relax, leaning back into the canvas seat and raising my feet onto the dashboard.

'You know what I'm looking forward to in Scotland?' I asked and continued without waiting for him to answer. 'Clear air. Big skies. The constant sound of running water from the River Ness. Spotting waterfalls along the way. Coffee and cake at I Should Cocoa, the coffee shop where I had a part-time job when I was in the sixth form. And swimming, of course.'

'Oh,' said Hector, non-committal.

I turned to gaze at his profile.

'Sorry, did you think I was going to say spending time with my parents?'

He took his eyes off the road for just long enough to cast me a mournful look.

'Actually, I rather hoped you were going to say spending a week of uninterrupted leisure with me.'

'Oh yes, that too. Plus, I'm really looking forward to showing you all my favourite places in and around Inverness: McNab's bookshop, the local park with the miniature railway, my favourite café, the River Ness, Loch Ness...'

'The monster?'

'You never know your luck.'

I settled down to enjoy the ride. As we negotiated the little maze of country lanes to take us to the motorway, the morning sun sparkled in a gentle autumnal way. Dewy emerald-green and chocolate-brown freshly ploughed fields ran in folds over the Cotswold hills like a crumpled patchwork bedspread laid over the fat curves of a sleeping giant. Hector sighed.

'In early autumn, the countryside around here is so beautiful. I'm beginning to wonder why we didn't choose a holiday destination closer to home'

I waved a hand dismissively at the landscape, radiant beneath the morning sun and a cloudless, clear blue sky.

'Just you wait till you get to Scotland. The hills north of the border are so magnificent, they make the Cotswolds look like speed bumps. And if you think our local sheep are cute, you'll be blown away by the Heilan' coos. That's Highland cattle to you, you great Sassenach.'

Hector braked at the junction at the top of Frocester Hill to give way to a tractor tootling along the main road.

'Are they the orange ones with the big tusks, like woolly mammoths?'

I laughed. 'Not tusks, silly. They're horns. But mammoth in scale, I'll give you that.'

We crossed the main road and passed through light woodland before starting our descent of the last Cotswold hill into the Severn Vale. The great river glinted in the distance, like a twist of silvery thread in front of the long, low, shadowy Welsh hills. Then Hector's mobile began to trill.

I sighed as I reached across to extract it from his top pocket.

'Not the shop calling already, surely?' He shook his head in silent apology as I pressed the green answer icon.

'Hello, this is Sophie; Hector's driving,' I said, expecting to hear Ted, and trying not to sound as irritated as I felt at our holiday being interrupted so soon. I hit the speaker icon.

'Sophie, darling, it's Kate.' Hector shot me a worried side-eye glance. 'Nothing to worry about,' she added quickly, as if psychically attuned to Hector's mood. 'It's just that I was looking for a book and I wondered whether you could help me.'

Hector rolled his eyes.

'Is that meant to be a Maggie Burton impression?' he hissed in a low voice, before saying loud enough for Kate to hear, 'Which book is that, Kate?'

'The one in Gaelic that was lying on the counter earlier,' she replied. 'So annoying, I know it was there when you came back in for scissors, and now it's nowhere to be found.'

Hector's brow furrowed.

'I've got it with me, Kate. It's in my jacket pocket. Why do you ask?'

The line crackled as the road dipped.

'Someone was after it just now. A fellow called into the shop just after you left. He'd heard you had it and was after it for himself. Really, Hector, I didn't know you'd already started up for second-hand trade. I thought you were waiting to do that when you got back. You might have briefed us about it.'

Hector frowned.

'Are you sure it's the same book, Kate? A collection of Gaelic poetry, in the original Gaelic. I don't understand how anyone would know I'd got it.'

'Does it have an inscription on the front page in the name of Malcom Nicolson?' asked Kate.

'Yes,' I replied.

Hector turned to stare at me in amazement, before an oncoming driver tooted his horn to indicate the Land Rover had strayed slightly across the central white line. Hector steered back within the lane boundary before replying.

'Was it someone local?' he enquired. 'Someone who'd seen the book on the trade counter? I wish I'd known there was a Gaelic speaker in the village. I'd have asked them to translate the inscription for me.'

Going through a mental roll call of our neighbours, I couldn't think of a single Scot.

'Oh no, he wasn't local,' replied Kate. 'He told me he'd just driven up from Clevedon.'

'Ah, that's a well-known Gaelic-speaking quarter of Somerset,' said Hector sardonically. 'I'm still puzzled, Kate. How did he know I had the book? I haven't listed it for sale online. We haven't put any of our second-hand stock in our online catalogue yet.'

That was a project for our return, once we'd decided exactly how we were going to operate Hector's new second-hand department. That was my brainchild as a new income stream for Hector's House.

'Apparently your mum put him onto you. She remembered you buying it at some car boot sale you visited with her earlier this year, and she gave him the details of your shop. She thought you'd welcome a customer for your new second-hand business.'

Hector paused as he negotiated the roundabout to join the M5.

'But that was back in January. How does he know my mum?'

Kate sighed. After all, she had only asked a simple question.

'I've no idea. What should I tell him then? He's just having tea and a bun in the tearoom while I locate it for him. And I've got someone else waiting to pay. Ted...' Her voice faded as she turned away to call him. A faint muttering suggested she'd stepped back to let Ted ring a sale up on the till.

'I'm sorry, Kate, not only is it not in the shop, but it's not for sale,' said Hector as we joined the motorway's inside lane. 'I'm taking it as a gift for Sophie's mum. Did you know she teaches Gaelic Language and Culture?'

'So what you're saying is it's *not for sale*.' Kate's voice boomed out across the ether, presumably as much for the benefit of the stranger in the tearoom as for us. 'Okay, I'll tell him.' She lowered her voice to a near-whisper. 'He was awfully keen, so perhaps I can interest him in that lovely new hardback of Robert Burns instead.'

'That's my girl.' Hector smiled in appreciation. 'Now, back to our holiday. Thanks for calling, Kate.'

I added a goodbye of my own before pressing the red icon to end the call, and I put the phone back in Hector's top pocket.

We'd only got as far as the sign indicating the first Gloucester turn-off when his phone pinged a message alert. I extracted it from his pocket again and speed-read the message before summarising to Hector.

'Kate says that guy's offered fifty pounds for the book, but she thinks he'd up his bid if you asked for more.'

I looked at Hector to gauge his response. He raised his eyebrows, keeping his gaze on the winding road ahead.

'Really? That's a pretty good mark-up, considering I only paid a pound for it at the car boot sale. Do you think I should ask for more?' He glanced at me for long enough to gauge my disapproval. 'I mean, I'm not suggesting we turn back to deliver it to him now. Our holiday will be short enough as it is, topped and tailed with this day-long drive. I guess if he's waited since

January to make his play for it, maybe another week wouldn't matter.'

I scowled into the distance, waiting, hoping for him to say the right thing. He got there eventually.

'I'm sorry, Sophie, no, he can't have it after a week either. I said this was a special present for your mum, and that's how it is. Can you text back a big "No" to Kate, please.'

I patted his knee in thanks, before tapping the message into his phone.

6

ROAD RAGE

A few miles later, Hector pointed to the sign for the second Gloucester turn-off. 'If we can't have a holiday in the Cotswolds, we should at least schedule a day out locally now and again. Gloucester Cathedral, now that's worth a special trip, and I bet you'd like to see the Tailor of Gloucester's shop. You know, as in the Beatrix Potter tale.'

I sat up straighter in my seat.

'Oh, yes please. That's one of my favourite Christmas stories. We'll be going through more Beatrix Potter territory soon, once we're past Manchester. We'll have some lovely views of the Lake District. But did you know that before her family started holidaying in the Lakes, they spent their holidays in Scotland, near Dunkeld in Perthshire?'

We fell into a long discussion about the life and work of Beatrix Potter, barely noticing the next few junctions, and soon we were passing Stoke-on-Trent.

'Hang on a minute.' Hector gripped the steering wheel more tightly. 'There's some idiot speeding up behind me. Why doesn't he just pull out and overtake if he's in such a hurry?'

We'd been pottering along at a steady sixty in the inside lane. Every time Hector accelerated beyond that speed, the vibrations became uncomfortable, and he slacked off just enough to abate them.

I leaned towards him so that I could see in the rear-view mirror what he was talking about. A small white van, somewhat dented at the front corners, had latched on, leaving barely a car's length between us.

'Maybe if you slow down a bit more he'll overtake,' I suggested. 'Or you could put your foot down to shake him off, to keep a safe stopping distance between the two vehicles.'

Hector smirked.

'Do I detect you've been swotting up for your driving theory test?'

I thought he hadn't noticed my recent purchase of a Highway Code study guide, which I needed to master if I were ever to pass my driving test.

'I think it'd be safer just to let him pass us,' said Hector, slowing down, but the van continued to sit on our tail. Fortunately, as we passed the entry ramp from the next junction, a long, high lorry managed to sandwich itself between us and the white van, so Hector put his foot down and we left him further behind.

I must have nodded off soon after that, because next thing I knew, Hector was prodding my waist with one finger.

'It's him again. I'd begun to assume he might be trying to tell me something, such as I had a faulty brake light, or I'd left my satchel on top of my car. But I know neither of those are true. I checked all the lights, the tyre pressures and the oil before we set off, like I always do before a very long journey. And I know I put my satchel on the back seat. I'm getting the impression that he's just being aggressive for the sake of it.'

'Maybe he's just got something against Land Rovers and enjoys winding up their drivers, same as some people do for caravanners.' I yawned and stretched before taking my feet off the dashboard. I stamped on the floor of the footwell to get the circulation flowing again. 'Just ignore him. That's the best thing to do with bullies.' I shifted slightly to relieve the pressure of the hard seat on my spine and turned to admire the Lakeland scenery.

'The hills are getting bigger,' observed Hector, nodding at the mauve-tinged fells. 'We've moved into Arthur Ransome territory while you've been asleep.'

'And Arthur Wainwright's.'

We kept copies of both the Lakeland's famous Arthurs' books in stock at Hector's House. To me the black-and-white line drawings of Arthur Wainwright's famous guides for fell-walkers bore little relation to the velvety slopes that surrounded us now, though I knew my father, as an experienced hillwalker, held them in high regard.

A blaring car horn made us both jump as the white van sped past us, before cutting in front of us so close to the Land Rover's front right wing that Hector had to slam on the brakes to avoid a collision.

The van's driver began to indicate left, before lowering his window and sticking his arm out, raising it up and down like a bird flapping its wing.

'Oh, for goodness' sake!' Hector muttered. 'What's he playing at now? Does that man have a death wish?'

'Are hand signals allowed on the motorway?' I queried, trying to remember the appropriate section of my Highway code primer. 'I don't even know what that one means.'

'Technically it means "I'm slowing down",' said Hector. 'But as he's doing it so close in front of us, I'd interpret it as meaning he wants us to pull over with him.'

'You should only stop on a motorway if you have an emergency, and then park on the hard shoulder, get out of the vehicle and await rescue on the verge, away from the flow of traffic.' That was one bit of the Highway Code that I was sure about. 'Or if a police officer pulls you over.'

'Well, he's clearly not a police officer, the crazy way he's driving, and even if he's got problems with his car, that doesn't constitute an emergency for us,' retorted Hector. 'It's never safe to stop on the motorway, anyway, even on the hard shoulder.'

He stepped on the accelerator and pulled into the middle lane, before gliding past the now stationary white van. I peered back at the driver, wanting to be able to recognise him if we encountered him again, but we were driving too fast for his face to be more than a blur to me.

Hector's eyes were on the rear-view mirror.

'Now he's pulled back onto the carriageway. I think he's going to try to catch us up. No, hang on he's slowing down again. His hazard lights are on, and he's moving over onto the hard shoulder.'

I craned my neck to catch a glimpse and clapped my hands in delight at what I saw.

'There's smoke coming out from under his bonnet!'

'Serves him right for being such an aggressive driver!' Hector grinned. 'Let's just hope he has a long wait before he gets rescued, so that we can be well and truly shot of him.'

Realising the tension had made my mouth really dry, within minutes I'd drained my water bottle.

7

FÀILTE GU ALBA (WELCOME TO SCOTLAND)

I crossed my legs.

'Hector, I'm really sorry, but we're going to have to stop at the next services.'

He glanced at the milometer.

'Which one will that be?'

This really wasn't what I'd intended.

'Gretna Green,' I replied in a small voice. 'Sorry. I'd hang on if I could.'

Hector shook his head. 'Don't worry. As long as you haven't a surprise wedding planned for me there, I don't mind stopping. I could do with a pee myself, as well as stretching my legs.' He wriggled in his seat. 'I haven't driven this far in one go for ages.'

'I'm afraid we've a lot further yet to go. We're not even half-way. I'm sorry I can't share the driving with you. It's an awful lot for one person to drive in a day.'

He patted the dashboard affectionately.

'I don't mind. It puts the old girl through her paces. She's probably glad of a decent journey. It makes a welcome change from my usual short trips dropping off book orders and running book fairs at schools and pottering up and down to see Mum and Dad in Clevedon.'

I pursed my lips. 'Are you sure you wouldn't like to marry your Land Rover while we're here?'

But before he could reply, I spotted the distinctive brown tourist information sign for Gretna Green's Old Blacksmith's shop. It was still a popular wedding venue for its romantic history, despite the marriage laws being uniform across the UK these days.

Then came the 'Welcome to Scotland' sign on the blue and white saltire with the Gaelic translation beneath: '*Fàilte gu Alba*'. My heart skipped a beat in my excitement at being back on Scottish soil and I raised my arms as if hurtling about on a roller coaster. 'We're in Scotland now!' I cried as the sign flashed past us.

Almost immediately we passed another brown sign heralding the turn-off for the Gretna Green Outlet Village, a modern shopping mall. I gritted my teeth at the overt commercial exploitation of a historic site, before reflecting that it must provide a lot of much-needed local jobs.

'Over the top,' murmured Hector, as he indicated left and entered the slip road for Gretna Services, with Ecclefechan to the west and Edinburgh to the east.

A meandering country lane led us to a spacious car park attached to a complex of shops and restaurants. It was a far cry from the famous but simple forge.

'Don't worry, Hector, Scotland's not all like this, I promise you,' I assured him.

Hector shrugged. 'No need to apologise. It's all new to me, sweetheart. My only knowledge of Scotland is through literature: *Dr Finlay's Casebook*, *Whisky Galore*, *Macbeth*, plus of course M. C. Beaton's *Hamish Macbeth* mysteries. I don't suppose Scotland's all like those, either.'

'A mix of those would provide an interesting holiday destination,' I observed. 'I know, let's wind up everyone back home by sending them a postcard from Gretna.'

'"Glad you're not here, Love Mr and Mrs Munro"?' replied Hector.

I was relieved we could joke about the thought of a Gretna wedding after all the cringing and teasing back home.

Hector relaxed even more when he spotted another Land Rover, exactly the same model as his, in the far corner of the car park, sheltered on two sides by high hedges. As if drawn by a magnet, he drove towards it and parked neatly alongside.

'Well, did you see that?' he declared as he applied the handbrake and switched off the engine. 'Looks like it belongs to a fellow bookseller! There's a sticker on the back window saying "Wigtown, Scotland's National Book Town".'

I opened my door, jumped down from my seat, and walked round the back to inspect our neighbour. The sticker showed a cute, colourful row of teetering old bookshops.

'Is Wigtown far from here?' asked Hector, coming round to join me. 'Can we make a quick detour?'

I folded my arms. 'Hector, anyone would think you were trying to put off meeting my parents.'

He looked a little sheepish.

'It's just that I've always wanted to go there. Besides, it would be helpful to chat to more second-hand booksellers to pick up their best advice. After all, although I'm experienced, I've only ever worked in new book shops.'

'Then you're in luck,' came a deep voice from the other side of the second Land Rover.

A mass of thick dark curly hair appeared round the corner of the vehicle, atop a friendly face with sapphire eyes and a chunky cable-knit sweater the colour of porridge.

I realised then that the driver had been crouched out of sight tending to his rear right-hand tyre. In his hands were an old-fashioned tyre-pressure gauge attached to a chunky metal foot pump.

'Hullo there, I'm Alasdair Graham, proud bookseller of Wigtown.' He got to his feet to greet us, offering a huge bear paw of a hand first to Hector, then to me.

'Hector Munro, proud bookseller of Wendlebury Barrow.' For a moment I thought they were about to exchange a secret handshake known only to those in the book trade. 'In the Cotswolds, down south,' he added, realising our new friend may not know where that was. 'I gather Wigtown is Scotland's answer to Hay-on-Wye.'

Alasdair raised a dark, well-shaped eyebrow. 'Aye, only far better.' His straight face crinkled as he let out a loud laugh. 'I'm only fooling. I've no' been there, ye ken. But if you've no' been to Wigtown, ye should. What's your speciality? Antiquarian? Rare books? Curios and collectibles? Between us, we've got the lot in Wigtown.'

Hector's shoulders hunched slightly. 'Until now I've been selling only new, but I'm looking to diversify into second-hand and vintage, curiosities too, if I can. But I could do with some pointers from old hands like you.'

'Ye heading our way? You can be there in under two hours.' Alasdair jerked his thumb westward. 'You're welcome to swing by any time for a blether.'

A sudden rustling behind the hedge made us all turn to look, but there was nothing to see.

'Actually, we're on our way to Inverness. My girlfriend's

parents have a house on the River Ness, and we're going to stay with them.'

'For a week,' I added. 'By the way, Hector, in Scotland, "stay" means you live somewhere. We're not going to live with them, just going for a short holiday.'

Alasdair smiled kindly. 'Aye, well, perhaps on your way back, if ye've time to spare, ye might wend your way to Wigtown. Come and bide a while in ma shop and I'll show ye the ropes. It's no' easy makin' a livin' this way, but if you're like me, it's the best way. So much more interesting to gather your own books to sell, rather than whatever publishers want to thrust upon ye. You'd be amazed at the treasures that come up at auctions and in house clearances. They're a speciality of mine, house clearances.' He nodded towards the back seat of his Land Rover. 'I just picked up a fine assortment of leather-bound Waverley novels. Not that many people read Scott these days, but the bindings and inscriptions set them apart. Just look at them!' He pointed through the window to the back seat of the Land Rover, where two big boxes, each holding two dozen books, were secured with the seat belts like precious children. 'Each one signed by the author. Just think, each touched by the hand of the great man himself, and who knows who else since then? It was worth the diesel from Wigtown for what I'll make from a collector, and the old dear was glad to see the back of them and more'n happy with the very fair amount I paid her for them, so a good deal all round.'

I peered through the window to admire his new acquisitions and noticed the neat inventory in a shaky hand that must have been the old lady's.

'I just stopped to adjust my tyre pressure before I head home as the old girl was pulling a little to the left. The Land Rover. Not ma vendor.'

Hector joined in his exuberant laughter, perhaps rejoicing at finding a kindred spirit. He reached into his inside jacket pocket and fished out a card.

'Here's my contact details if you're ever down our way, Alasdair. We'd love to see you anytime. Otherwise, let's connect online.'

Alasdair reciprocated, extracting his own card from his back jeans pocket and handing it over.

'Aye, same to you.' Then he glanced at his watch. 'But I must be on ma way as soon as I've set ma tyre to rights. I've a darts match tonight. So long for now, Hector and Sophie, and enjoy Inverness. Make sure you look up McNab's while you're there. You're in for a treat there. Isn't that right, Sophie?'

'Aye,' I replied, so pleased that he was including me that I came over all Scottish.

We left him crouched down by the faulty tyre, unscrewing the little plastic cap to apply the nozzle of the foot pump.

As Hector and I strode hand in hand across the car park to the toilets, there was a distinct spring in Hector's step, although his legs must have been weary after the long drive so far, and I realised he was marching in time to the sound of bagpipes emanating from the forecourt.

After a quick visit to the shop to buy postcards – for Carol to reassure her, and for my elderly next-door neighbour Joshua, who was feeding my cat Blossom while I was away, as well as for the gang in the shop – we grabbed a cup of coffee and an Ecclefechan tart in the café.

When we returned to the car park a little later, shifting from foot to foot beside Hector's Land Rover was a man of about forty, with neat, slicked-back honey-coloured hair, smart in a navy blazer, red tie and grey trousers. From his anxious demeanour and the name badge on his lapel, I guessed he was the centre manager or other official, about to tell us off for parking in the wrong place, or something similar. Then I spotted a couple more smartly dressed types in name badges nearby, erecting barriers to prevent cars entering or leaving the car park.

Hector stopped abruptly, put his arm round my shoulders to bring me to a halt, and spun me round to face back towards the visitor centre.

'Don't look, Sophie,' he said in a hoarse voice. 'But I think something awful has just happened to our new bookseller friend.'

8

SLIGHTLY FOXED

I broke free of his grasp to swing round and look, and promptly wished I hadn't. Sprawled on the tarmac between the two Land Rovers was the felled figure of Alasdair Graham. A dark-red pool was spreading over the car park's bumpy surface, framing his curly hair. I covered my mouth with my hand, regretting the Ecclefechan tart.

'What on earth?' I began, but before I could say any more, a police car, followed by an ambulance, sped round the corner from the lane, lights flashing and sirens blaring, and screeched to a halt at the impromptu barriers. One of the centre staff ran over to remove the cones to let them through, before replacing them as soon as the vehicles had passed through. It seemed we were now in a closed site.

Transfixed, we stayed where we were, conscious of a crowd gathering around us. A couple of paramedics leaped down from an ambulance and darted into the gap between the two Land Rovers, obscuring our view. A police officer meanwhile began to affix crime scene 'do not enter' tape to portable lightweight posts, fencing off both Land Rovers plus an additional margin of about two metres. A second police officer disappeared between the vehicles. All we could see was the paramedics' yellow and green high-visibility jackets moving, as presumably they tried to revive poor Alasdair.

Speculative murmurs rippled through the crowd. I heard the visitor centre's automatic doors click as they locked behind us to prevent any more tourists joining us in the car park. Those trapped inside pressed their faces up against the glass, craning to see what the fuss was about.

'Were they together, do you think?' said a member of the public behind us. His Yorkshire accent marked him out as a tourist. 'Were the two Land Rovers travelling in convoy?'

'Was the dead man on his own?' asked a Liverpudlian. 'I thought I saw him talking to a blonde girl as I was parking.'

'No, it was an old lady,' replied his companion. 'Or an old man. Someone with grey hair and walking stick, in any case.'

I nudged Hector.

'Do you think we should approach the police and tell them we spoke to Alasdair just now? We may have been the last person to speak to him.'

I swallowed the word 'alive', hoping it wasn't necessary.

Hector squeezed my hand in encouragement.

'I'd give them a bit longer,' he suggested. 'Perhaps wait until they've cleared the scene first. I'm not sure we've got anything useful to tell them. It's not as if we noticed anything suspicious. But all the same, I'm sure they'd want to speak to us.'

The chatter behind us was swiftly silenced by the sight of the paramedics returning to their ambulance for a stretcher. Another burst of speculation was quashed as they emerged a few moments later from between the Land Rovers with what was clearly a dead body on the stretcher, completely covered by a blanket, face and all.

A groan of sympathy and a few cries of horror rang out. Hector dropped my hand so that he could put both his arms around me. I buried my head on his shoulder and let my tears fall in silence as he stroked my hair.

Just then a second police car arrived, heading for the crowd of spectators rather than the scene of the crime. Well, the scene of the accident at least. 'Don't go to meet trouble halfway,' old Joshua, my next-door neighbour liked to say, and his voice rang in my head now. Alive until proven dead. Tragically, I didn't have to wait long to meet this particular trouble.

The officers in the second car acted quickly to subdue and disperse the crowd. The manager unlocked the doors and tried to shepherd us all back into the building. A disembodied voice asked us over the tannoy to form an orderly queue to give our contact details to centre staff. My heart sank at the realisation that their questioning could considerably delay our journey. I quickly berated myself for putting our needs before poor Alasdair's.

To my surprise, Hector, usually so law-abiding, held back from following the crowd indoors. He still had his arms around me, so I could hardly stride ahead, leaving him behind. Then I realised he was hanging back to speak directly to the police, rather than to the centre staff.

The female officer approached us quizzically, and Hector advanced towards her, pulling me with him.

'Hello, Officer, I think my girlfriend and I here might be able to offer you useful information about the...'

He hesitated, raising his eyebrows in an unspoken, delicate question.

'The deceased, sir, yes, I'm afraid so. Was he a friend of yours?'

'Only of about half an hour's standing. You see, I parked

beside him, having spotted he was a fellow Land Rover aficionado, and when we got chatting, it turned out we had even more in common.'

He repeated Alasdair's description of himself, his hometown, his shop and the reason for his journey.

'Do you think the attack was for robbery?' I put in. 'He told us he had valuable old books on his back seat. Perhaps a book thief knew about them and was after them.'

'He said he'd make a profit on their resale,' said Hector. 'But I doubt that would be a big enough profit to justify murder. Besides, it seems unlikely that a casual thief staking out the car park would be able to spot a valuable old book at a glance.'

'Not that any amount of money would justify murder, sir,' the officer reproved him.

Hector cleared his throat. 'No, sorry, of course not. I meant to tempt a man to commit murder, not to justify it.'

'But it might be worth checking all the books are there, in any case,' I persisted. 'Or might one of them have been used as a murder weapon? Maybe his assailant used it to give a fatal blow to his head.'

The police officer flashed me an uncertain look.

'How did you know about the blow to the head?'

I took a step backwards.

'I just guessed. I couldn't think how else a book might be used to kill someone.'

The police officer considered for a moment, before turning her back on us to radio her colleagues over by the Land Rovers. After they'd exchanged a few sentences, she returned her attention to us.

'No, miss. It appears someone's rifled through the books rather carelessly, but they're all intact and unblemished, and there are none missing from the handwritten checklist that was with them. Besides, no book would have been heavy enough to cause that sort of blow.' She gave a mirthless laugh. 'My gran used to swear by an old folk remedy you may have heard of, that if you have a ganglion on your wrist – that's a sort of fleshy lump – it will disappear if you bash it with the family Bible, but I've never heard of one being used to kill someone.'

I let out a squeal of inspiration.

'Wait! I know what the murder weapon was. Or what it might have been, at least.' I tugged at Hector's sleeve. 'Hector, do you remember what Alasdair was doing when we arrived? What he had in his other hand when he greeted us?'

Hector looked blank, so I turned to the police officer. 'He was adjusting the pressure in one of his tyres.'

The police officer hesitated, her finger over the screen of the tablet on which she'd been making notes.

'Don't people usually do that on a petrol station forecourt these days when buying fuel?'

Hector shook his head. 'Not if you're the sort of person to enjoy tinkering with Land Rovers. Then you'll probably be the type to carry out little maintenance tasks at your leisure, wherever you are.' He looked at me for a moment. 'I remember now, sweetheart; he had an old-fashioned metal foot-pump in his hand, the sort with a built-in tyre gauge. If someone applied the corner of that to a human skull with any force, it wouldn't do them any good at all.'

We all winced at the thought.

The officer took a few steps away from us to radio that intelligence to her colleagues, who then began searching the hedges that bordered two sides of the van.

Hector rubbed his chin thoughtfully.

'If the murderer was lurking in the bushes ready to pounce, he'd be long gone by now. Your sirens will have sent him packing. We could hear them for some time before you came into sight on the approach road to the car park.'

'Oh my,' murmured the officer, then, more volubly, 'so did you notice anyone hanging around nearby while you were talking to Mr Graham?'

I glanced at Hector before speaking.

'Not, but there was substantial rustling going on in the hedge beside us at one point, far more than would be caused by a sparrow or other local wildlife. Don't you recall, Hector? We all turned to look at it at one point, but we couldn't see anything unusual.'

Hector covered his mouth with his hand, and I closed my eyes.

'Oh my goodness, Hector, why didn't we look more closely? We might have uncovered the villain, and Alasdair would still be alive now.'

The officer laid a hand gently on my shoulder.

'Now, now, miss, please don't distress yourself. You'd only stopped for a comfort break, I presume?'

I nodded feebly.

'Well, then, you could hardly be expected to be on the lookout for crazed attackers. I mean, this isn't exactly the rough end of Glasgow. As far as you were concerned, this was a safe, family-friendly tourist attraction. You've been very helpful, more helpful than most here will be, I'll bet. Now, let me just take your contact details, as we may well need to call on you to sign a written statement and maybe even to act as witnesses for the prosecution somewhere along the line. Then you will be free to continue your onward journey.'

As she glanced over her shoulder, we noticed one of her colleagues was now dusting Alasdair's Land Rover for finger-prints. I guessed Alasdair had left it unlocked while he was checking the tyre pressure. Perhaps the keys were still in the ignition, where he'd left them, expecting to drive away a few minutes later.

Another police officer was on his back inspecting the underneath of the vehicle. Surely they weren't expecting to find the attacker clinging to the chassis?

'Perhaps before you get behind the wheel again, sir,' the first officer was saying, 'you'd better make time for another cup of tea. You both look as if you could do with one. But would you mind leaving your keys with us while you do, in case we need to move your vehicle to a parking space further away? I'm sure we'll still be here on your return.'

'Of course, Officer. Thank you. And if you need to check it over at all, you have my full permission.'

Once we were out of earshot of the police, I said in a low voice to Hector, 'What did you say that for? Do you really want them fingerprinting your Land Rover too?'

'Rather that than have them present us with a search warrant,' he said evenly. 'After all, we know we've got nothing to hide.'

* * *

Half an hour later, we returned to the car park, dawdling to put off the dreadful moment of encountering the murder scene at close quarters. Thankfully, Hector's Land Rover had been moved away from Alasdair's, and now stood on its own in the middle of the car park. As we approached, a male police officer in a white plastic coverall stepped over the crime scene tape to greet us and return Hector's keys.

'You'll be pleased to know we found nothing amiss with your vehicle.'

Hector bridled.

'Pleased and not remotely surprised,' I replied before he could speak. 'We had nothing to do with poor Alasdair's death. As I said to your colleague earlier, if you want to find the murder weapon, I suggest you look for a tyre pump.'

Hector tugged at my hand as a hint to stop talking.

'Thank you, Officer. So, may we go now? We have to reach Inverness tonight and we're keen to press on. Your colleague has our contact details for when you need us to sign a statement, and no doubt you've logged my licence plate as well.'

The officer nodded assent.

'One moment, sir, and I'll lift the barrier for you to leave. You can be on your way, miss. Just leave the investigation to the lads now.'

At this sexist remark, I wanted to pull a face at his back when he turned to remove the barrier, but I thought it best not to antagonise him. Even so, I couldn't help but feel triumphant when, as I turned for one last look at the sombre scene, one of his colleagues emerged from the hedge, holding aloft the bright red metal tyre pump that I'd last seen in poor Alasdair's hands.

9

_____

ONWARD AND UPWARD

We re-joined the motorway in silence and drove on for a few miles, both deep in thought, before either of us spoke.

'I'm not sure I should have mentioned my view that the average car park thief wouldn't recognise the value of old books,' was Hector's opening gambit. 'I bet their first thought was, _No, but a fellow bookseller would_. I might as well have held up a sign saying, "number one suspect".'

I waved his concern aside.

'We know you're innocent, so that hardly matters. Besides, you're not an expert in second-hand books yet, just a hobbyist collector. It's not as if you're already running a successful second-hand book business that would have competed with Alasdair's.'

He took a little comfort from that thought, and I continued.

'And had you considered, Hector, that although he told us he was a bookseller, that might have been a cover story? He might have had quite a different reason for his journey. I remember thinking when we went to park beside him how odd it was that he'd parked so far away from the entrance to the café area – as far away as it was possible to be without leaving the site.'

'Perhaps he just wanted a quiet spot to make a phone call,' Hector suggested. 'Or he was shy and craved the privacy that those hedges provided. He'd driven into the parking space, rather than reversing, so when he was in the driver's seat, he would have had his back to anyone passing by.'

I frowned.

'He didn't seem the shy type to me, though. Don't you remember how cheerful and extroverted he seemed when he came over to introduce himself? And he did have a Wigtown sticker on his rear windscreen, as well as two boxes of old books on his back seat.'

'Yes, but anyone could put a sticker like that on their wind-screen, a reader as readily as a retailer. The sticker doesn't prove a thing. There are loads of bookshops there, and it's unlikely he'd meet someone here that knew them all. Let's think. What else do people go to car parks for, if not to use the local services? Dodgy dealings from their cars? Drugs? Fake designer handbags and watches?'

I sank down in my seat. I'd really liked Alasdair and didn't want to believe he was in any way shady.

'He seemed too healthy for a junkie. His hair was glossy, his skin clear.'

Hector slowed down slightly to allow a huge, juddering Royal Mail lorry to pull in front of him, its red livery vivid against the dull green hills beyond, like the pimento inside an olive.

'One might argue that if he was truly in the habit of driving about the country to source stock from house clearances, he'd have his shop's name and contact details emblazoned on the side of his vehicle for a bit of free advertising,' he said. 'You don't pay VAT on commercial vehicles, you know.'

I considered for a moment.

'Then why haven't you got your shop's name on your Land Rover?.'

'I didn't buy mine new. You only get VAT relief on new vehicles.'

'That's no excuse. It's still free advertising once you've paid for the decal. If Hector's House – or Alasdair's shop – was my business, that's what I'd do.'

Hector laid a hand gently on my thigh.

'Let's not talk shop for a bit, Sophie. This is meant to be a holiday. Time for us to be just a couple enjoying time off together, rather than employer and employee.'

He was right, of course. That was the purpose of the trip, after all – to present ourselves as a couple to my parents. It was unfortunate that Alasdair happened to be a bookseller, or at least was pretending to be one, as we'd got this far on our journey without talking about the business, since dealing with Kate's phone call. Even more unfortunate, to say the least, that Alasdair had been murdered. Which led me on to another train of thought.

'If you're right about the bookseller story being a false front, maybe he wasn't even a Scotsman. I mean, didn't he seem like the archetypal Scot to you? Almost a cartoon Scot, with his "ayes" and "ye kens" and "blethers"?'

'I thought the hackneyed stereotype of a Scotsman was a redhead with blue eyes and a dour manner. Not a... What was his colouring again, Sophie? You're better at noticing these details.'

I lifted Hector's hand from my thigh and clasped both my

hands around it. Would Alasdair's hands have been cold by now? 'He had dark hair that fell into natural curls and green eyes and—' My voice broke for a moment. 'Now that I think about it, he actually looked very much like you.'

Hector's other hand slipped on the steering wheel, and we swerved slightly, causing the driver of the Ford Mondeo overtaking us to sound his horn. Hector pulled his left hand free of mine to signal an apology.

'Really?' he said a moment later. 'I don't remember thinking he was my doppelgänger.'

'I hope he wasn't,' I said, raising my feet onto the seat and looping my hands around my knees. 'You know what the old doppelgänger legend says: meet yours and you die.'

'Well, sadly, Alasdair has died now.' Hector laid a hand on my knee. 'Maybe the legend only applies to one of you, rather than wiping out both at once in a kind of deadly game of Snap. But tragic as it is for poor Alasdair, we mustn't let this crime blight our first holiday together. Can we please change the subject? We want to be in good spirits when we meet your folks.'

He was right about that. I wanted him to get off on the right foot with my mum and dad. Although I generally wished they lived closer to me, just now I was glad that we still had a couple of hundred miles ahead of us in which to process this tragedy.

'Best not to tell Mum and Dad anything about Alasdair,' I suggested. 'I don't want to make Mum any more anxious than she is already.'

Hector nodded, and we drove on in companionable silence as the road began to rise through scrubby rolling hills the colours of a bruise, on which shaggy sheep lurked in the shadow of deep green pine plantations.

This engaging, constantly changing scenery did not stop me

wondering whether Alistair had a girlfriend waiting for him at home, or a wife and children, who might just now be hearing the tragic news of his demise from a police officer who had turned up unexpectedly on their doorstep.

wandering wheresoever Alistair had a mind to roam, and was not at home in a wild and children, who might that now be braving the bugle news of his demise from a police officer who had rung frightened spouse...

10

TAKING THE HIGH ROAD

'How did you ever bring yourself to leave?' asked Hector. 'It's so beautiful up here. It feels like we're driving through the sky.'

He leaned back in the driving seat, enjoying a little more leisure to appreciate the rolling Highland scenery now that we were on the A9 beyond Perth, with barely another car in sight. Slowly and steadily, we climbed the high road that connects the populous agricultural centre of Scotland with the more rugged and remote northern Highlands.

'When you're eighteen years old, and you've grown up amid stunning scenery, you take it for granted, and a pretty landscape doesn't provide you with what you really need at that age: further education, life experience, new horizons, independence. Look around, Hector.' I waved my arm to take in all around us. 'Do you see much there to fulfil a teenager? That's why I headed south of the border to university.'

He changed down a gear to cope with a steeper stretch.

'You weren't tempted to head back after you'd finished your degree? Surely there would have been jobs for you in Inverness?'

I grimaced.

'I did have a job there while I was at school, waitressing in my favourite café, I Should Cocoa. But you'd hardly call it a career.'

A bit like my job at Hector's House tearoom, I thought, frowning.

'But after university, most of the jobs available were in leisure or tourism, and lots of them only lasted for the summer season. I didn't want to skulk about at home doing nothing all winter. The winters are long and dark up here, you know, with an hour's less daylight at either end of the day than in the Cotswolds. It'll be dark by six o'clock now in Inverness, when it's light until seven in Wendlebury.'

I twisted round to haul the cool bag off the back seat and onto my lap. Mrs Wetherley and Ted had kindly packed a surprise picnic for our journey, which they presented to us as we were packing our final bits and pieces into the Land Rover. We'd started on it while we were still on the M5, but the Ecclefechan tarts – and the murder – at Gretna had suppressed our appetites for the rest of it until now.

'So, you went off to teach English abroad instead?'

I nodded as I unwrapped a couple of Ted's delicious sour-dough rolls, stuffed full of Carol's best Gloucester Old Spot ham. I handed one to Hector before taking my first bite of mine, buying time to frame my answer. I'd taught English while joining my then-boyfriend Damien as he took his travelling English language theatre company on a never-ending tour of European capitals.

'Eventually.' I hoped my clipped tone implied that I didn't want to talk any further about that part of my life. Only after I'd left Damian had I realised how unhappy I'd been, allowing Damian to dictate where and when I could work, and subsidising his struggling theatre company's takings with my teacher's salary.

Another brown tourist sign came into view.

'Look, that's Dalwhinnie, Scotland's highest distillery. Have you ever been to a distillery? I think my dad's been to all the distilleries in mainland Scotland. We should visit one while you're here. But not necessarily with my dad.'

As we progressed, I turned into Hector's personal tour guide, giving a running commentary on the attractions indicated on the brown tourist information signs. I swallowed the last bite of one of Mrs Wetherley's excellent jam tarts.

'It would be pretty desolate, albeit in a grand sort of a way, without these fancy places punctuating the landscape,' said Hector. 'How odd to choose to live in one of these isolated cottages that we keep seeing in the middle of nowhere. If they weren't painted white, we might not even spot them.'

I helped myself to an apricot flapjack.

'Especially on a dreich day when the hills are shrouded in mist,' I agreed.

'They put me in mind of the crofter's cottage in the old black-and-white film of John Buchan's *The 39 Steps*,' said Hector. 'You know, where Private Frazer from *Dad's Army* is married to Peggy Ashcroft, and she helps Robert Donat escape the policemen chasing him across the moors.'

'John Laurie, you mean.'

We'd been watching a lot of old films together lately, and I'd chosen *The 39 Steps* as an overture to our trip up north, along with *Monty Python and the Holy Grail*, filmed at Doune Castle, a *Harry Potter* for the glimpse of the Glenfinnan Viaduct, as well as Diana Gabaldon's *Outlander* series, filmed all over Scotland.

'Of course, we've Sir Walter Scott to thank for popularising the Highlands among the English,' continued Hector. 'Not that many people read his books today, although a fine bound set might still appeal to a collector.' When he stopped speaking abruptly, I realised he was thinking of poor Alasdair again, with all those Scott novels on his back seat. I'd never read any of Scott's novels, and I thought it would be a very long time before I would even consider it after today.

'The Highland Outdoor Heritage Museum!' I cried, pointing at another brown sign, grateful for the distraction. 'It's an outdoor museum of social history, with old buildings moved here and reassembled or recreated here. An *Outlander* film set, too. If we can fit it into our week up here, I'd love to take you there. It's only an hour's drive from Inverness.'

Just as it was starting to feel as if we'd be driving along this high, sparse road for ever, we began to spot signs of modern civilisation and then the urban sprawl of Inverness, its city lights twinkling in the early evening darkness. Even the increase in traffic was welcome after spending much of the last couple of hours seeing barely another vehicle. Then, appearing on the horizon like the Emerald City of Oz after Dorothy's trek along the Yellow Brick Road, was Inverness itself, calling to us via the motorway exit sign, to enter the winding slip road that would carry us to the coast road along the Moray Firth.

As we began to pass industrial estates and edge-of-town retail outlets, Hector harrumphed.

'This is not how I pictured Inverness at all.' His face clouded in disappointment. 'I thought Inverness would feel like a village, but this feels like a city.'

'Of course it's a city, with its own cathedral. And a thriving one too, the fastest growing city in the UK, according to my dad. But a city bounded by the Beauly and Moray Firths, with the Black Isle to the north, edged by the Great Glen, and a stone's throw from Loch Ness. Hardly your average city. Anyway, don't be so selfish. All these services that we're passing are essential to locals. People come from as far as the Western Isles to use them. It's the only development of its size in the Highlands. Surely you don't begrudge Highlanders the same kind of services that we have down south?'

'Sorry,' said Hector. I quickly forgave him.

'Anyway, I'm very glad we're here at last. It hasn't been the easiest journey, what with that awful business at Gretna, not to mention that idiot in the white van.'

Hector's jaw relaxed a little.

'After what happened at Gretna, I don't know why you're letting that stupid driver upset you still. He was probably just some idiot with a grudge against Land Rover drivers. You get them sometimes, the same way that you get people honking at cars towing caravans or motorhome drives. Small-minded people with empty lives or an incurable case of envy.'

He patted the dashboard affectionately, as if wanting to reassure his Land Rover that he still loved it despite all it had been through today.

With my back stiff and my bottom sore from our long drive, I didn't mention that I'd have no hesitation in swapping this spartan vehicle for a luxury motorhome, given half the chance.

'Follow the road round to the right,' I instructed as we passed a couple of superstores. 'Then bear left, and we'll soon be beside the River Ness.'

'Do we have to cross the river?' asked Hector as we approached Ness Bridge.

'No, go straight ahead at the traffic lights, then we're nearly there.'

As the lights turned green, I wound down my window and took a deep breath of fresh Highland air. I held it in my lungs for as long as I could, before exhaling in a contented sigh.

'Just smell that air, Hector! Did you ever smell fresher? Now, turn left at Faith, Hope and Charity – that's the Three Virtues statue in front of us – or else you'll end up on the footpath.'

A moment later I was guiding him onto the forecourt of an imposing Victorian house that throughout my teens I'd called home.

As soon as he'd pulled on the handbrake and switched off the engine, I jumped down onto the gravel, then turned back to see why Hector hadn't yet opened his door too. Surely he should have been keen to get out and stretch after such a long drive?

'Come on, we're here!' I called unnecessarily, impatient to greet my parents.

Hector had turned slightly pale.

Before I could chivvy him any further, the front door of the house flew open, and my parents came bounding out.

'We heard you parking,' said my dad, with a side-eye at the Land Rover. My dad drove an ancient red sportscar, an MG BGT. It was his consolation prize to himself when I left home and would no longer be calling on him to provide taxi services to me and my friends. The Land Rover towered over both the MG and my mum's more practical, midnight-blue Mini.

I threw myself into Dad's arms for one of his customary bear hugs, my eyes misty with unshed tears. I hadn't realised how much I'd missed him. Then I moved onto my mum, who, once we'd finished hugging, couldn't resist straightening the collar of my shirt and tucking a stray strand of hair back into my ponytail.

Hector, now standing by the open door of the Land Rover – at least he'd deigned to get out during our family reunion – cleared his throat, and I went to grab him by the hand and drag him over to meet Mum and Dad.

'Hello again, Hector.' Dad held out his hand in welcome and

gave Hector's a hearty shake. 'So pleased to meet you under happier circumstances than last time.'

'Yes, the only previous connection we've had with you was May's funeral,' added Mum. 'Let's start over, shall we? I don't want to keep associating you with death.'

Hector gulped.

'So, did you have a good journey, love?' Dad was saying as he turned to lead us into the house.

'Smooth and uneventful, thank you,' said Hector, squeezing my hand in secret complicity.

As he spoke, I realised that in the year and a bit since I'd moved to Wendlebury, I'd encountered more deaths or near-deaths than in my entire life before then. I pulled my hand free of Hector's on the pretext of retying my ponytail, then let him pass through the front door before me. As I turned to close the door behind me, I heard the screech of brakes just beyond our house. I stepped back out onto the path to peer along the road to find the source of the awful noise and saw a small, scruffy white van pulling into the kerb. Common sense told me that it couldn't possibly be the same van that had been harassing us on the motorway, but even so, I slammed the door more heavily than necessary and all but ran into the front room, where I was glad to accept the glass of sherry my father had just decanted for me.

11

A DRAM TOO FAR

After our welcome glass of sherry, I couldn't resist taking Hector through the house to the back door, down the garden path, and out onto the riverside walk.

'Good lord, do you think we should throw that man this life preserver?'

He pointed to a guy in green chest-high waders standing in the middle of the river with his back to us, then to the orange-and-white buoyancy aid mounted in a wooden case on a stake beside the river.

When I laughed, he shot me a puzzled look.

'Well, I don't want to add a drowned man to our list of holiday casualties.' He took a step forward to lean against the low barrier installed to stop pedestrians from straying onto the steep, slippery riverbank. 'One dead body is one too many, and we've had that already.'

I suppressed a smile, feeling guilty for being amused so soon after poor Alasdair's demise.

'He doesn't need rescuing, silly. He's enjoying himself. Look!'

The man standing in the middle of the River Ness had his

back to us, and now he turned round to reveal the fishing rod held out in front of him.

'See, he's got chest-high waders on. This is a popular fishing spot.'

Hector emitted a small sigh of relief.

'Anyway, you can see why fishermen like it here, can't you?'

I stretched my arms out in both directions to share my feeling of space and freedom.

'Just breathe in the clear air,' I enthused. 'So clean and fresh and invigorating; I'd like to bottle it and take it away, so I could top up with a quick sniff whenever I was missing this beautiful place. Honestly, Hector, there's no air like it.'

He breathed in tentatively.

'The air's free, you know,' I continued. 'Don't you welcome it after being stuck inside the Land Rover all day?'

I pointed to our left.

'Look, that's Ness Islands down there – two little islands in the middle of the river. It's a lovely spot for a romantic stroll. And across there,' I pointed across the water, 'is the swimming pool and the ice rink. And further down is Whin Park, with its boating lake and miniature railway. Oh, and the crazy golf course. We'll have plenty to fill our week, even if we don't go far beyond the city.'

Hector scratched his head.

'So where's the famous Loch Ness? I kind of thought we'd be able to see it from here.'

I slipped my hand into his.

'Oh no, that's further south. It's a short drive away, but the best way to see it is by boat from the pier at the edge of town. I'm always happy for an excuse to take the boat.'

'And the famous bookshop that Alasdair recommended?'

I pulled on his hand to spin us round to face down river

towards the city centre. 'Not far from Ness Bridge, where we turned left earlier. It's an easy walk from here. We'll go tomorrow morning if you like.'

I was sensing it would be psychologically wise to take him into one of his comfort zones when so much was new and strange to him. After all, Scotland is a whole different country.

A bicycle bell sounded shrilly behind us, and Hector pulled me back against the wall to let it pass. It was rather nice to be on a path free of motor vehicles after all that driving.

Then we went through to the front of the house and out of the front door to fetch our bags from the Land Rover.

'Oh, thank goodness, it's gone!' I said without thinking, as Hector handed me my backpack from the boot of the Land Rover.

'What's gone?' he asked, extracting a small carrier bag partly filled with bubble wrap.

I hesitated, wondering whether to invent a troublesome insect, such as a spider on the parcel shelf, rather than tell him the truth.

'Oh, nothing,' I said, unconvincingly. When he eyed me with suspicion, I knew I wasn't going to get away with that. I slung the backpack over my shoulder and fetched our coats from the back seat. 'It's just that when we arrived, I thought I saw that tatty white van that was pestering us on the M5, and it unnerved me. But don't worry, I can't see it now. If it was there, it's gone now.'

Hector shouldered his own bag and slammed the Land Rover's rear doors. He looked up and down the street.

'You're worrying about nothing, sweetheart. There must be thousands of vans like it in the country. It seems highly unlikely that one would follow us all that way. Even the most aggressive motorist would be unlikely to expend all that time and fuel pursuing another vehicle to the far end of the country just for the sake of road rage.'

'Not quite the far end,' I corrected him. 'It's another three hours' drive further if you want to go to John o'Groats.'

'Anyway,' Hector persisted, 'if you recall, the last time we saw him, he had smoke pouring out from his engine, so I doubt he made it much further.'

We headed back into the house, dropping our backpacks at the foot of the great wooden staircase that rose four storeys above us. Mum came out of the front room, from which she'd pointedly removed our empty sherry glasses after just one drink.

'I've put you in the back bedroom on the top floor so you'll have the best view,' she said. 'But before you unpack, there's a nice drop of soup keeping warm for you on the stove. I don't know when you last ate, but you must be ready for something hot inside you. I hope you don't mind, but Dad and I had ours earlier.'

'That's fine, Mum,' I assured her. 'It's way past your usual teatime, nearly bedtime, in fact.'

We followed her into the kitchen where the big old deal table was set for two, a plate of oatcakes at the centre of the table.

'So how many bedrooms are there here?' asked Hector as we sat down. 'It's a huge house.'

Mum was spooning a chunky Scotch broth into two earthenware bowls.

'Eight, officially, when it was a hotel, but they're not all bedrooms now,' said Mum. 'It had gone out of business, surprisingly for its location, which is what sold it to us. There are a few other benefits that are hangovers from its trading days – locks on every window and an extensive burglar alarm system.'

When I was a teenager, forgetting my key, I'd frequently

cursed the security system, but in my current state of anxiety, I was grateful for it.

'You look tired, love,' said Mum, setting my bowl of soup in front of me. 'Hardly surprising after that long drive. And for such a short stay too, barely a week. Do you really have to go back so soon?'

'Sorry, Mum, but Saturdays are the busiest days in the book-shop, and Hector didn't want to miss more than one.'

'Then why didn't you just fly up from Bristol, like Auntie May used to do? We could easily have picked you up from Inver-ness Airport, or you could have got the shuttle bus into the city centre. It would have made much better use of your time away from the shop.'

The steam rising from the soup was warming my cheeks and sending a peppery fragrance into my nostrils.

'Maybe next time,' I said, picking up my spoon.

Mum raised her eyebrows, but said nothing, leaving us to eat our supper alone.

'Don't take it personally, Hector,' I said in a low voice after she'd gone. 'All forms of travel make her nervous these days. If we'd flown up, she'd have asked us why we didn't come by car.'

After we'd finished eating, Hector pulled the Gaelic book from his jacket pocket.

'I nearly forgot,' he said, holding it up to show me. 'Shall I give it to her now?'

As we passed through the hall, he also extracted from his backpack a long, thin gift bag that I hadn't realised he'd stowed in there. I led him into the snug where my parents were sitting in matching armchairs either side of the fire, Dad reading the local newspaper and Mum an ancient hardback without a dustjacket, so I couldn't tell what it was.

'Hector's brought you each a little present,' I announced, turning to Hector.

Hector presented Mum with the little book.

'I thought you might find this interesting.' He opened it at the frontispiece to show her the handwritten inscription. The dark-blue ink looked paler in the dim light of this windowless room.

Mum moved her coffee cup on her side table to set down the book she was reading and took the Gaelic poetry book from Hector.

'An inscription always adds interest and value to a vintage book,' he said, eager to please her. 'Although the inscription here looks considerably more recent than the book itself. Not modern exactly, but not brand new either. Shame there isn't a date on it.'

Mum lowered her glasses and opened the book to read the inscription on the frontispiece. 'So it looks like a gift from a Malcolm Nicolson – to himself? No, to his son or grandson, I reckon, who had presumably been named after him. It's an extraordinarily long inscription.'

'Do you think it was a birthday or Christmas gift?' asked Hector.

'If the inscription looked older, I'd say that was unlikely. In the strictly religious Gaelic-speaking communities, as in the Outer Hebrides, birthdays used to pass unmarked. They were considered decadent. Even so, if the book was presented for a special occasion, you'd think the giver would have added the date. But it's not exactly a congratulatory message of goodwill, more of a rant, telling the recipient off for his dissolute lifestyle which he says is impoverishing him. I'm not sure whether he means spiritually or financially, although both would work. This little book, he says, will restore his soul and make him rich in the only way that truly matters.' She looked up and smiled at Hector for the first time. 'It's the sort of book that might be allowed as Sunday reading, however, as an alternative or supplement to the Bible, as the theme of the poetry is devotional. Although often the family Bible was the only book in the house, and for those evicted in the Highland Clearances, it was sometimes the only possession they took with them, apart from their clothes. If you don't mind, I'd like to take this to work with me tomorrow to show to my colleague, Ross Blair. He divides his time between the university and the National Archive Office just along the river there, and he'll know better than me whether this kind of inscription is unusual or particularly noteworthy. He should be on campus tomorrow, so I'll take it with me to ask his advice.'

Hector smiled, gratified. 'It's your book to do what you like with, Mrs Sayers.'

'Shona, please.' Mum smiled back. 'And my husband's Gordon. Thank you, Hector, that's a very thoughtful and original gift. It will sit well in my collection of Gaelic books.' She pointed to the floor-to-ceiling bookshelves fitted into the alcove on her side of the fire, each one bearing a title in Gaelic. A matching set of bookshelves on my dad's side of the fireplace was filled with his Ordnance Survey maps and books about hillwalking and the geology of Scotland.

I was relieved on Hector's behalf that Mum had been so pleased with his gift, but my nerves jangled when he presented the long, thin gift bag to Dad. Dad pulled out a bottle of Hector's favourite brandy. I hadn't known he was planning to give something also to my dad, or I'd have advised him against anything alcoholic. Dad already drank far more than was healthy.

Dad raised the crystal tumbler that was already in his hand.

'I'm more of a whisky man myself, Hector, but I'll never say no to a drop of decent brandy.'

He set his tumbler on the side table beside his folded newspaper, took the bottle from Hector and examined the label.

'You'll never say no to a drop of anything,' murmured Mum. I closed my eyes to shut out my embarrassment.

Dad chuckled. 'So is this meant to be a dowry, son? Is there something you wanted to ask me?' He winked at me.

'Dad!'

Sensing my embarrassment, Mum did her best to salvage the situation.

'It's enough for us that you were a friend of my husband's aunt,' she said quickly. 'She always spoke very highly of you, Hector. She was so impressed with the fact that you managed to set up a thriving bookshop in such a small village, and she told us how supportive you were of her books, too.'

Still stiff from so many hours in the Land Rover, I stretched my arms above my head, flexed my back, and yawned.

'Actually, Mum, I think we'd better go and unpack now, because if I sit down on the sofa in front of the fire, I'll fall straight to sleep.'

I bent down to loop an arm around her shoulders and kiss her on the cheek before doing the same to my dad.

'Lovely to have you home, love.' Dad put a hand on my back to prolong my embrace. 'Shall we see you in the morning before we go off to work?'

I glanced at Hector, whose eyes were drooping with exhaustion.

'We'll sleep until we wake to get over the journey, if that's okay, and restore our strength for the busy week I've planned for us. There's so much up here that I want to show Hector.'

Dad patted my back.

'Okay, love, you do what you think best, and we'll see you when we get home from work tomorrow, which won't be a moment too soon.'

As I stood back from his chair, he grasped my hand and gave it a squeeze.

'Sleep tight, the pair of you.'

It was only as I straightened up that I spotted the half-empty whisky bottle on the floor beside Dad's chair.

12

A SCOTTISH BREAKFAST

Next morning, waking before Hector, I swung my legs round to haul myself out of bed and tiptoed onto the landing to listen out for sounds of my parents. I wasn't sure what time they'd be heading for work – it varied each day according to their academic timetables – and after the slight awkwardness of the night before, I wanted to ensure Hector had enough time to wash, dress and recover from the journey before spending more time with them.

I soon realised that the rest of the house was in silence, and that Mum and Dad must have left already. Even so, I crept downstairs to avoid waking Hector and set some coffee brewing in the kitchen before dropping a potato scone into the toaster.

I'd just spread some of Mum's bramble jelly on my toast when I heard Hector's tread on the stairs. With three flights to descend, I had time to toast another scone for him and to collect an earthenware mug from the shelf of the dresser for his coffee by the time he entered the kitchen.

He'd already dressed, apparently shy of presenting himself to my parents in his pyjamas, and his curls were slightly limp, still damp from his shower. I glanced down apologetically at my nightie and dressing gown – an ancient tartan one left over from the old hotel, which had hung courtesy robes on the back of every bathroom door. Sized to fit even the largest guest, it reached my ankles.

'Your hair will just have time to dry off before it gets wet again when we go swimming,' I said, setting his coffee in front of him.

Hector's eyes widened.

'Isn't it a bit cold for swimming? It's noticeably colder than at home.'

'Hector, it's never too cold for swimming.'

I caught his scone as it popped up and watched him spread it generously with pale unsalted butter and the glossy, dark jelly, all the more shiny against the matte surface of the cold butter.

'That book we had in the shop on wild swimming,' he began. 'It cautioned against the cold water until you've become acclimatised to it. We're only here for a few days. Surely we won't have time to acclimatise?'

I rolled my eyes.

'I'm not talking about wild swimming, which, in any case, we just call swimming in this house. Where did you think I was planning to take you?'

Hector pointed a wavering finger towards the back of the house.

'Good heavens, not in the River Ness. It would be freezing, and far too fast. I was thinking of the corporation pool across the way. It's got brilliant water features, slides and all sorts. You'll love it.'

Hector clapped his hand to his forehead as if he'd just remembered something.

'Sorry, Sophie, I've no trunks. Remember? Still, never mind, you said there's plenty else to do here.'

I wasn't so easily deterred from visiting my favourite indoor pool.

'No problem, we can divert into town first and pick up a cheap pair at the budget clothes shop on the High Street. It's only just up from Ness Bridge. And if they don't have any, they always have them for sale on reception at the swimming pool.'

Hector's face clouded. You'd think I'd offered him the choice between a firing squad and a guillotine. I guessed he wasn't as keen a swimmer as me, but then the world would be a dull place if we all liked the same thing in equal measures. However, I sensed the need to soften him up a little.

'And while we're in town, we can pay a quick visit to McNab's, the huge second-hand book emporium that I've told you about. Just a quick visit, mind, to whet your appetite. You could easily spend all day there. We can go back again later in the week if we have time.'

He smiled at last. 'Now you're talking.'

As he tucked into his second scone, I headed upstairs to get dressed and to stuff my bikini, shower gel, and shampoo into my tote bag. Popping into the snug afterwards to collect the spare key from its usual hiding place, inside the green majolica vase on top of the piano, I noticed that Mum had left Hector's book on the side table beside her armchair. Had she left it on purpose, annoyed by his gift of alcohol to my dad, or was it by mistake in her hurry to get to work? Either way, I decided we might as well take it into town with us to get Mr McNab's opinion on it. If he thought the book was highly valuable or of historic interest, it might get Hector back into Mum's good books.

When I suggested this to Hector, he perked up, slipped the book into his pocket, and slung his satchel over his shoulder. Then we headed into town along the riverside walk.

13

STAIRWAY TO HEAVEN

On the High Street, Hector couldn't get out of the clothes shop fast enough. With his new black swimming trunks stuffed into my bag, we left the store and headed towards the edge of the city centre, passing various bars, restaurants and charity shops, in the direction of McNab's Bookshop.

On the way, I stopped only to show him the fascinating Old High Church, with its connections to the tragic Battle of Culloden.

'The victorious English army imprisoned captive Scots soldiers in the church tower before bringing them out to be shot,' I explained as we strolled hand-in-hand around the historic churchyard. 'See that little reddish stone with the groove in the top? That was where the executioner rested his musket to take aim. And those stones beyond are where they made the prisoners kneel, their backs to the musketeer.'

I felt Hector shudder.

'All in the shadow of the church,' he murmured. 'Still, I suppose it was practical for their burial.'

I shook my head sadly.

'Unfortunately they didn't bother burying them. Instead, they left their bodies outside in the street for their families to collect.'

'Ugh, how appalling.' He put his arms around me and hugged me close.

'Local legend has it that if you come back at night, you'll hear ghostly children singing in the churchyard,' I went on. 'Young victims of the plague, I suppose. But don't worry, I won't bring you back here after dark.'

We stood in silence for a moment to show our respect for the dead. Then Hector rallied a little.

'So, where's this famous bookshop that you keep promising me?'

I smiled.

'Not far now.' I was looking forward to seeing his rapturous reaction. 'I'm sure it will give you plenty of ideas for how to run your new second-hand department.'

When we finally reached the door of the converted chapel that housed the McNab's Bookshop, with remarkable self-restraint, Hector held the door open for me to go in first, and as he followed me inside, I swung my arm up dramatically.

'Ta da!' I crowed, proud on Mr McNab's behalf to be introducing him to such a legendary shop.

Once across the threshold, Hector stood still, open-mouthed, and gazed around the store. It must have contained tens of thousands of books, if not more, crammed onto shelves from floor to ceiling at ground level, with more again around the gallery that ran all around the building above our heads. Where a section had more books than shelf space, the surplus books were piled high on the floor, waiting their turn to fill gaps made by customers' purchases. At the sales desk at the centre of the room, old Mr McNab, dressed in an ancient beige Fair Isle sweater, sat engrossed in a novel, partly concealed behind a wall of books that ranged around the counter top. Nearby, a large wood-burner crackled cheerfully. Towering above the fire, an ornate, wrought-iron staircase spiralled up to join the gallery, raising our eyes heavenward. Against the wall at the back of the shop, a straight staircase provided an alternative route up. The shop was a veritable maze to delight any book lover, not least Hector.

'What time do they close?' he asked in a low voice, moving towards the shelves nearest the door as if planning to work methodically around every section.

I laughed.

'We're not staying here all day if that's what you're thinking.'

He'd already pulled a book off the shelf, opened it and begun to read.

'Half an hour here, tops, then we'll head off for our swim, okay?'

He nodded, entranced, and I left him to browse while I went off to find the travel section, eager as ever to look for books by my Auntie May.

When I was a child, I used to be concerned when I found her books in charity shops or Little Free Libraries, thinking they were doing her out of her royalties. May soon put me straight.

'If someone who doesn't know my work finds one of my books second-hand for a pound, they're more likely to take a punt on it than at the full retail price of the same book brand new. Then, if they like it, they'll often seek out more, most likely buying them new, so I'll probably earn royalties from them eventually. It all helps grow my readership, as well as democratising reading. Not everyone can afford to buy books when they're brand new.'

It wasn't until I was older that I understood what she meant and recognised her generosity. She didn't want poverty to prevent anyone from enjoying the benefits of reading.

So, I was delighted to find a whole shelf of her work on the mezzanine, and I sat down cross-legged on the floor to work my way through them all, checking the price of each one to gauge its market value and looking for interesting inscriptions. It was often fascinating and rewarding to read affectionate recommendations from giver to receiver, and this time I was overjoyed to find a copy of her slim volume about staying as a guest in a convent inscribed by my aunt to a Sister Francis. I couldn't help but wonder how Sister Francis had borne parting with it. Had she left the convent? Had it closed down? Had my aunt made the gift without realising the recipient had taken a vow denying herself earthly possessions? If so, perhaps the Mother Superior made Sister Francis sell it to raise funds for the convent community.

I was so engrossed in my speculations, flicking through the book to look for any tell-tale notes left by the reader, that I didn't for a moment recognise the sound of Hector crying out in alarm. When a harsh metallic jangling resonated from the centre of the vast room, I rose stiffly to my feet to emerge from the travel section and peer over the iron balustrade that edged the gallery. To my horror, sprawling on the rag rug at the foot of the stair-case lay Hector with an elderly lady kneeling beside him, her hand on his brow. A much younger man was kneeling on the other side of Hector, putting a strong arm around his shoulder to help him sit up. Mr McNab rushed out from behind the counter to investigate. In the background somewhere, there was a flurry of steps across the parquet floor, then the front door slammed closed, presumably some rogue taking advantage of the distraction to make off with a book without paying.

Everyone was too preoccupied with Hector's well-being to take any notice of the sneaky shoplifter.

Still clutching the nun's book, I ran along the gallery to the top of the stairs and hastened down them, hanging on tightly to the handrail to make sure I didn't tumble down on top of the prostrate Hector. Mr McNab glanced up at me in alarm.

'Steady, dear! Don't do what your man has just done. I'll be having words with Morag if she's been too zealous on the stairs with the floor polish.'

He returned his attention to Hector, who was now raising himself to his feet and dusting down his jeans. The elderly lady, with some effort, bent to pick up a familiar-looking volume that lay face down on the floor a metre away from Hector's feet.

'Mr McNab, you shouldn't leave books lying around where a body can trip over them, you know. Is that what made you fall, son?'

Mr McNab took the book from the elderly lady and flipped it open at the front cover, looking at the top right-hand corner of the first page where he usually pencilled his prices. He shook his head.

'It's not one of mine, Mrs Murdoch. My price mark isna there.'

Hector reached out to reclaim the little book.

'No, it's mine. I came in here with it tucked away in my pocket. I know I took a bit of a tumble, but I must have turned a cartwheel for the book to fall out of my pocket of its own accord. It was a tight fit.'

I coughed as I came to stand beside him. He took the hint.

'Actually, it's my girlfriend's mother's book. We just brought it in to show you, hoping you might be able to shed light on its value and significance.'

'Well, there's no need to throw yourself down my stairs to

bring it to my attention, laddie. A simple request at the counter would have done.'

When I laughed, Mr McNab looked at me and did a double take.

'Why, if it's not young Sophie Sayers! How's your mum, dear? And your faither?'

I smiled, pleased that he'd remembered me even though I hadn't set foot in the shop for over a year. It had been a regular haunt in my school days. If I hadn't spent all my wages in I Should Cocoa, I'd bring what was left to blow on an old book.

'They're both fine, thanks, Mr McNab.'

'I was so sorry to hear about your faither's old auntie last year, the travel writer,' he continued. 'You can tell your folks she's still as alive as ever in this shop, and still as popular, if not more so.' He lowered his gaze. 'I'm sorry to say this, but, as any bookseller will tell you, one of the best things an author can do to boost sales is to drop down deid.'

I nudged Hector gently.

'Don't go getting any ideas, Hector. You're worth more to me alive than dead.' I put an arm round him tenderly, wary of potential injuries.

Mr McNab looked at him with interest.

'Are you a travel writer too, sir? Will I have heard of you?'

Hector's smile was apologetic.

'Actually, I write novels under a female pen name. Pot-boilers, really, to subsidise the finances of my bookshop. I'm a bookseller by trade myself, down in England, in the village where May Sayers was based. She was a good friend and mentor of mine. In fact, she helped fund the shop when I opened it a few years ago.'

Mr McNab raised his eyebrows bushy enough to provide nests for small birds. 'What kind of a shop? New books or old?'

'All new at the moment, but I've a large private collection as a start-up stock for a used books department I'm planning to open.' He cast a hand about him. 'There's certainly plenty here to give me ideas. You have a wonderful shop here, sir.'

Mr McNab nodded approval. 'Good luck to you, son. If you ever need advice, just give me a bell, and I'll see what I can make of it for ye. Now let's start with a look at this little curiosity of yours.'

I laid a hand on Hector's arm to detain him before he followed Mr McNab.

'Are you sure you're OK, Hector? No bones broken? No damage done?'

Hector gave a sheepish grin. 'Only to my pride. Now, let's consult the expert about your mum's book.'

I dropped my hand and let him follow Mr McNab to the counter, where they perched on adjacent stools to read the inscription. As there was no third stool, I left them to it and wandered over to the romantic fiction section to look for the works of Hermione Minty.

14

HONOUR AMONG BOOKSELLERS

'It was very kind of Hamish to give you May's book for free,' said Hector, beaming, as we left the shop a little later. I'd known Mr McNab for years and still called him Mr McNab, whereas Hector had met him less than half an hour ago and was already on first-name terms with him.

It had taken a while for me to lure Hector out from behind the trade counter, where I suspect he was pretending the shop belonged to him.

'Hmm, more likely a canny Scot seeking to avert the risk of you suing him for damages. But you're right, he needn't have done it. It's not as if it was the cheapest of May's books on his shelves. He'd marked it up for twenty pounds, and it'll be worth a lot more if the nun that she signed it for is featured in the book. I'm going to read it to find out.' I took Hector's hand as we waited at the traffic lights to return to the riverside path. 'Perhaps I should write something up about it for the Hector's House website, or maybe write an article to sell to a magazine or newspaper. Then we could use the article to promote your new second-hand department. Not that I want to sell it, but I don't mind loaning it to you for display purposes only – same as Mum is thinking of doing with the Gaelic book, if a museum wants it. You could get a little glass case to display curiosities and rarities, and books that are too fragile to put on a normal shelf.'

Hector squeezed my hand in encouragement.

'Then maybe once a month I could write a blog post about each new display. Or we could give show-and-tell talks in the shop, with wine, after hours, to generate business for the new department.'

The lights turned green for us to cross, and we strode briskly across the road towards the river. I was pleased Hector's fall didn't seem to have done him any obvious harm. It could have been so much worse. If he'd broken an arm or a leg, he wouldn't have been able to drive us back to Wendlebury Barrow. Yet another indicator that I really ought to learn to drive. I'd put off learning while I was with Damian, knowing that if I could drive, he'd end up volunteering me as chauffeur for his theatre group, but I knew Hector would never exploit me like that.

I pulled on Hector's hand. 'Turn right across Ness Bridge, then we'll head down the far riverbank to the swimming pool.'

Hector halted for a moment, grimacing, to flex his spine and roll his shoulders. Perhaps I'd been too hasty in giving him a clean bill of health.

'Hector, just how many of those stairs do you think you fell down? I didn't see you fall. I only heard the sound effects. Did you fall all the way down or just the last few steps?'

He frowned as he arched his back. 'At least half, I'd say.'

I shuddered.

'I've never felt safe on spiral staircases. I always hang on tight to the handrail just in case I miss my footing.'

Conscious that we were blocking the narrow pavement

across the bridge, I slipped my arm through Hector's and nudged him to start walking again.

'That's the funny thing, though, Sophie. I swear I was holding on to the handrail, but then I went flying. It wasn't you messing about, was it? You didn't sneak up behind me and give me a shove for a laugh, did you?'

'No, I didn't even realise you'd come upstairs to join me. I was too preoccupied in the travel section, checking all of Auntie May's books for interesting inscriptions.'

'So that's where you were. You must have been hidden behind some of those piles of books on the floor. I couldn't find you and I was just going downstairs to look for you there.'

'Anyway, why would I push you downstairs?' I made a feeble attempt at humour for the sake of his bruised ego. 'It's not as if I've got you insured.'

Hector shrugged. 'To hurry me along to your beloved swimming pool?'

'Of course not. So, who was it then? Did you see anyone behind you?'

'To be honest, I was too busy trying to break my fall.'

I replayed the scene in my head.

'Wait, I remember hearing the rapid scurry of footsteps towards the door, just as people were gathering around you to make sure you were all right. Perhaps whoever shoved you darted to the far end of the gallery and down the straight stairs to the ground floor, then ran out of the shop and slammed the door before anyone could accuse them. It was as if that person couldn't get out of the shop fast enough. At the time, I assumed it was an opportunistic shoplifter, but perhaps it was your attacker making a dash for it. What do you reckon?'

Hector shook his head.

'Actually, I don't suppose whoever that was had anything to

do with my fall, sweetheart. I expect I just caught my toe in the ornate ironwork and tripped. My legs are stiff after that long drive yesterday, and I was probably so lost in admiration at the amazing sight of all those shelves full of old books that I wasn't looking where I was going. Ooh, is that Inverness Cathedral up ahead?'

I was not so easily distracted from my sleuthing.

'Yes, it is. But you're usually so sure-footed. Even if you didn't see anyone behind you at the top of the stairs, did you hear footsteps behind you? Or perhaps the sound of someone breathing close at hand? As you descended the staircase, did you feel any vibrations that would suggest another person's tread in your wake? Although if they'd kept in perfect step with you, you might not have noticed. The staircase is pretty rigid, not like the wobbly footbridge across the Ness.'

As we crossed the road at Ardross Terrace, I was seized by an impulse to check for scruffy white vans and glanced about us, but there were none in sight. Not that there were many on-street parking places round here. If the attacker had come into town in his van, he'd have had to find a car park. I tried to put the van out of my mind and continued. 'It would be easy for an attacker to dash out of the shop and make their escape while everyone's attention was turned on you. Not that you'd have been able to identify them even if you saw them, provided they'd kept behind you the whole time and weren't acting suspiciously. You didn't see me even though you were actively looking for me.'

Hector let out an enormous sigh.

'Look, can we just drop it? I tripped up and made a spectacle of myself, and I'm embarrassed. You got a free book out of it, and I befriended Mr McNab, so it's all good. There's no need for you to make excuses for my ineptitude. It was just a momentary lapse of attention, that's all. Can we just forget it now, sweetheart? Please?'

'Ok, if you sure you're not hurt.'

I pointed to the sign for the cathedral's café.

'How about we stop for a cup of tea and a sandwich, to calm us both down, and maybe have a look around the cathedral too, before our swim?'

When I patted the swimming bag that hung from my shoulder, I noticed that my bikini top was hanging over the side, suspended by a single strap. I wondered how long it had been like that, grateful not to have lost it. That explained how Mr McNab had known to call out, 'Enjoy your swim!' as we were leaving the shop.

'It's a nice Victorian cathedral, so not that old, but with some interesting features that I think you'll like. Let's go inside first, then over lunch you can tell me what Mr McNab said about Mum's book.'

Hector brightened.

'I thought you'd never ask.'

15

SANCTUARY

'My mum always does this for her best friend,' I said in a low voice as I used a taper to light a votive candle on the black candelabra. I held it up for a moment to gaze into the tiny flame, saying a prayer for Mum and Dad in my head. We stood back to admire the effect of the flickering lights in this shady corner.

'Is her best friend very ill?' asked Hector, his voice gentle in sympathy.

I didn't take my eyes off my candle's flame, wishing with all my heart that Mum's friend was still alive.

'No, don't you remember me telling you about her? Suzy, the friend who drowned in the sea while Mum was asleep on the beach.'

I tore my gaze away from the candelabra to give him a quizzical look. He was usually such a good listener. I couldn't believe he'd forgotten already.

Hector coughed, embarrassed.

'Oh, yes, of course. I'm so sorry, Sophie. When you said her best friend, I just pictured someone who was still alive. Or maybe I'd suppressed that story, not wanting to think about someone drowning just before we have our swim. What an awful way to die. Avoidable, too.'

'Only up to a point. Tragically, even the most experienced swimmers with the best knowledge of wherever they happen to be swimming occasionally get caught out. Mum feels responsible for her death still, although no one has ever blamed her in the slightest.' I fumbled in my tote bag for my purse and dropped another coin in the box to pay for a second candle, before lighting it and setting it on the stand. 'This candle is for Suzy.'

Hector rubbed his nose.

'But no one makes people go wild swimming,' he insisted, a little heartlessly, I thought.

I folded my arms so that he couldn't hold my hand.

'No, but sometimes people just want to immerse themselves in nature, to find themselves there. The world seems a different place after you've viewed it from the perspective of a swan. Others do it to rise to a challenge, to push themselves to the limits. Don't you think the world is a better place because of people like that? Who dares, wins.'

'And fools rush in.'

I was beginning to wonder whether he might be slightly concussed. He wasn't usually so unsympathetic.

He slipped an arm round my shoulders.

'Come on, sweetheart, let's not argue. Now let's go and have that lunch.'

I allowed him to draw me closer, but I kept my arms folded as we left the cathedral and headed for the café in the cathedral yard.

He winced as he set the tray of tea and ham sandwiches on our table before lowering himself carefully onto his chair. He caught my eye as I looked him up and down.

'Actually, Sophie, I think the bruising from my fall just now is already starting to come out. Perhaps we'd better give swimming a miss today.'

I poured our tea and added milk.

'Oh, but a good swim is just what you need. A nice soak in deep water taking the weight off your body. Hydrotherapy is a thing for a reason, you know.'

Hector stared mournfully at his ham sandwich. Perhaps he'd fallen further and landed more heavily than I'd realised. I'd only seen him after he'd landed.

I couldn't help thinking that whenever I'd slipped on a stair before, as soon as I felt myself falling I'd grabbed the bannisters. Hector usually had fast reactions and excellent balance. Why hadn't he done the same?

Perhaps he'd had no advance warning. I glanced at his feet to check his footwear. His stout suede lace-ups had a very deep tread. He couldn't have slipped in those. He must have been pushed.

Pushed by a stranger from the top of the stairs. He must have guessed we'd be too preoccupied with checking Hector for broken bones to pursue him. He'd probably also have guessed that we wouldn't have associated him with Hector's fall until much later, by which time he'd be a long way from McNab's bookshop. But why would someone push Hector?

Needing more time to think about that theory before I pressed Hector further about his fall, I steered us onto a cheerier topic.

'So, what did Mr McNab say about Mum's book? Did he tell you your gift is worth a fortune?'

He brightened a little.

'Not in itself. I'm afraid the book is pretty common. He

wasn't interested in buying it. He has a dozen other similar copies of it in his shop already and hasn't sold one for ages.'

'That's good news, then. So, if that guy who wanted to buy your copy is still interested, he can order one from McNab's.'

Hector nodded.

'Yes. I don't know why he didn't just look it up online in the first place rather than drive all the way from Clevedon to Wendlebury. It's strange, also, that he waited from January when I bought it until now in September. It can't have taken that long to trace my shop.'

I topped up our tea from the teapot.

'Maybe he's internet averse or a bit dim. Not everyone likes shopping online.'

'No, that's true. But anyway, back to what Mr McNab was telling me. He says that, as with that book of May's he gave you, the inscription might make this particular copy of interest to social historians. It looks as if it's a message from father or grandfather, or maybe uncle to son, grandson, or nephew. He agreed with your mum's translation and elaborated on it a bit. He said it's a moralising rant admonishing the recipient against breaking the Sabbath, for serving drink and gambling instead of God as his master and chasing loose women. Mr McNab thinks there are a lot of Nicolsons on Lewis, so it may well come from there. In the olden days, they were very strict about keeping the Sabbath on Lewis.'

'Oh, yes, Mum's told me all about that,' I said.

Hector stared into his tea for a moment.

'Do you know, I'm wishing I showed this book to Alasdair now,' he said, his voice breaking. 'I thought we were rather getting on. Poor Alasdair.'

Until Hector had mentioned Alasdair, I hadn't associated his murder with the incident in McNab's shop.

I leaned closer to Hector and lowered my voice.

'Hector, this might sound absurd, but it's just occurred to me that perhaps someone out there has a grudge against book-sellers and is hunting them down. Having accomplished his mission with Alasdair, maybe he's now in murderous pursuit of you. Maybe that's why he pushed you down the stairs just now.'

Hector set down his cup with a clatter and gazed at me, open-mouthed.

'Perhaps we should warn Mr McNab,' I continued. 'Perhaps the attacker will come back for him next. He'd be easy pickings, cornered behind his counter with nowhere to hide.'

Hector reached across the table to cover both my hands with his.

'Come off it, Sophie. You're letting your imagination run away with you. I'm sure it was just me being clumsy. No need to make a big thing out of it, honestly.'

But I was beginning to wish I had lit candles for Hector and Mr McNab too.

16

AFTER THE FALL

'So, if you weren't pushed, what do you think made you fall?' I asked Hector as we strolled beside the River Ness towards the swimming pool complex. 'Or are you going to tell me you were reading a book as you went down the stairs and not looking where you were going.'

When Hector tutted, I bit my lip. I was beginning to sound like my mum.

'Sweetheart, I'm not five years old. Of course I wasn't reading a book. Nor was I running with scissors. I suppose I might have been a little distracted by the vision of all those books around us, but not enough to make me forget I was walking down a spiral staircase. Although I confess I don't know how to account for my fall. I'm usually very sure-footed.'

That was true. I'd seen him positively run up and down ladders, putting books on the highest shelves in his shop. Nor did he have a fear of heights that might have made him feel woozy enough to fall.

'Do you remember feeling anything as you fell?' I didn't want to suggest anything too specific for fear of planting a false memory in his head.

He smirked. 'Feel anything, Sophie? What, you mean like my life flashing before my eyes or my late grandparents calling my name, telling me come towards the light at the end of the tunnel?"

'No, I didn't mean that sort of thing. But did you feel anything unexpected?'

I uncrossed my arms and looped my hand through the crook of his elbow.

'No, of course not. Nor did I have an out-of-body moment hovering up near the ceiling, watching people grieve over my broken body.'

We turned inland and, leaving the river behind us, strolled past the shinty field towards the imposing modern building at the far end of the road.

'What I mean is, do you remember feeling, perhaps, a hand on your back? Not a helping hand, or someone just trying to get your attention, but a shoving hand.'

'Oh look, mini golf,' cried Hector, nodding towards the sign on the left. That was a desperate attempt to change the subject. He usually concurs with Mark Twain – that golf is a good walk spoiled.

'Never mind the mini golf. Just give me a straight answer, and I'll stop asking. Do you think you were pushed down the stairs?'

The corners of his mouth twitched.

'Are you confessing, Sophie? I didn't have you down as a practical joker.'

'I'm no such thing!' To be honest, I'd rather his assailant had been me in a moment of ill-judged pranking than a malevolent stranger who might still be on his trail.

I glanced behind us, suddenly fearful of being followed.

There was no one in sight, just a squirrel romping across the grass between two trees.

Hector jiggled my hand in admonishment.

'Look, I don't know why you're making such a fuss about this, Sophie. I tripped, I fell, but I lived to tell the tale. I might be a bit bruised and shaken up, but as my grandmother used to say, if you can feel pain, it means you're still alive. It could have been a lot worse, but it was hardly the Eiffel Tower that I fell down. Just a small flight of steps in a cosy, safe shop.'

I decided not to mention that in a Golden Age detective story I'd once read, *Murder Must Advertise* by Dorothy L. Sayers (no relation), a man plummets to his death down just such a flight of stairs, landing with a broken neck, dead before he hit the floor.

'Anyway,' Hector continued, 'if I'd been seriously hurt, an ambulance would have been there in no time. Didn't we just pass a hospital?'

'Yes, and a hospice for the dying.'

We walked on in silence until Hector tried to lift our mood by pointing to the flat-topped hill that lay beyond the pool complex.

'So is that one of your dad's Munros?'

'No, silly, it's far too small to be a Munro. It's Tomnahurich Hill, home to a Victorian cemetery.'

I grimaced. Death seemed to be everywhere we went on this trip, following us like the Grim Reaper.

But as we ascended the sloping path to the swimming pool admissions desk, my spirits began to lift. Our next destination would be completely safe. Not only did lifeguards patrol the entire pool complex, but video cameras were trained on all the public areas too. There was no hiding place, except perhaps for the changing cubicles, but that was only reasonable.

What's more, this was going to be my first swim since I'd got back from Ithaca in May, and it could come not a moment too soon. A nice swim would soothe my frayed nerves, relax my tense limbs, and restore Hector's equilibrium after his unfortunate but very minor accident.

17

ALL CHANGE

Once we'd paid for our swim and received bright red wristbands in return, we headed for the changing area. A few minutes later, we emerged from our cubicle in our swimming costumes, stuffed our clothes into adjacent lockers and fumbled to lock them with tiny keys on orange rubber wristbands. Before I could slip mine over my hand, I dropped it on the wet floor, and Hector, ever chivalrous, bent down to pick it up and handed it back to me. He winced at the pain in his back as he straightened up, but I pretended not to have noticed. I was impatient for my swim.

As we walked towards the pool, I looked sideways at Hector, clocking the neat fit of his plain black swimming shorts.

'From the waist up, you'd make a great merman,' I said, slapping his bottom playfully.

Hector grinned. 'Are you fishing for compliments, you siren? You're not so bad yourself.'

He rested his hand on the small of my bare back as we rounded the barrier to the shallow pool full of fun water

features. Then I steered him off in the direction of the competition hall.

'Let's warm up first with a few lengths in the competition
pool. I haven't had a proper swim for ages, and you can't do
lengths in the leisure waters because they're an irregular shape
and don't have lanes. They're also a lot shallower.'

'Sure,' he said, sounding anything but sure.

As soon as we reached the poolside, I dived in and began
ploughing up and down enthusiastically like a duck kept too
long from the farm pond. It was only when I paused after my
first six lengths that I realised Hector was still hovering, bone
dry, on the poolside, at the point from which I'd entered the
water. As I surfaced to catch my breath, he crouched down on
his haunches to talk to me. I wondered whether his back had
been too stiff to allow him to dive in after me.

'I didn't know you were part dolphin,' he said, scraping my
wet hair out of my eyes. I smiled, gratified.

'Yes, I've always been a water baby. My mum used to take me
swimming all the time before Suzy's accident. I could swim
before I could walk.' I sensed he wasn't keen to join me in the
competition pool, and I didn't want to embarrass him by forcing
him if he was unwilling for whatever reason. 'Let's go to the
leisure waters now.'

I hauled myself out of the water and playfully gave him a
dripping wet bear hug. That earned me a whistle and a
reproving shake of the head from a sombre-faced lifeguard
seated at the top of a ladder. 'No petting,' he mouthed. In mock
penitence, I lowered my hands to my sides.

'Do you know what my favourite thing about swimming is?'
he asked, taking my hand as we waded into the fun pool, whose
entry point sloped as gently as a beach.

I sucked in my tummy, wondering whether he was about to

compliment me on the bikini I'd bought especially for this trip. For swimming outdoors I usually favour a more practical one-piece.

'People-watching,' he said, looking everywhere but at me. I let my tummy muscles relax. 'Swimming pools are like soap operas, with little dramas going on in every corner. Being a life-guard might seem like a boring job, but it must be fascinating to speculate on everyone's backstories, watching relationships flourish or fail in the water.'

We were waist deep by now, and I leaned forward to start a leisurely breaststroke towards the far end. Hector followed, still walking rather than swimming.

'I mean, look at that couple over there.' He indicated a pair of teenagers tightly locked in each other's arms. 'I was surprised that a lifeguard didn't blow a whistle at them for indecency, but the lifeguards here seemed younger and less stuffy than by the competition pool.

'They're not here for the good of their health, are they? And that dad over there, trying hard to keep his daughter happy. I bet he's divorced, and this is something he does with his little girl as an access visit. And as for that couple, in the Jacuzzi, well, they should just get a room.'

I laughed. 'Oh, stop being such a novelist and just enjoy the exercise. Come on, Hector, this is lovely. The water's so warm, and, being term-time, the pool's relatively empty.' I flipped over on to my back and floated, spreading out my arms and legs into a star shape and closing my eyes for a moment. 'Isn't this bliss?'

Hector, now chest deep, ventured to go horizontal, grasping the end wall and allowing his legs to float up behind him. Just then a klaxon sounded. Clearly alarmed, Hector lowered his feet to the floor, still firmly gripping the ledge.

'What's that? A fire drill in a swimming pool? Surely not.'

I glanced across to the wall-mounted board with flashing lights that indicated which feature was about to start up.

'They're just about to turn on the wave machine,' I said. 'Come on, this is a good time to go over to the rapid river feature, while everyone else jumps up and down in the waves. I prefer doing gentle circuits of the rapid river anyway.'

'A dolphin that doesn't like waves?' said Hector. 'There's a novelty.'

I swam ahead of him, as fast as I could, standing upright only when I had rounded the corner and entered into the oval channel that housed the rapid river feature. The pool alternates its machinery: waves on, rapids off, and vice versa. The waters were relatively still here now, but it was still fun to swim round the circuit, or to float in the huge rubber rings provided as buoyancy aids.

I turned to face Hector as he waded to catch up with me. 'I know it's silly when the waves here are completely under control, but that machine still makes me feel sick when I think of the current that carried Suzy to her death.'

I grabbed two large colourful rubber rings as they floated towards me and slipped one over his head and the other over mine. We laid our arms on top of them and kicked our legs behind us.

'I'll swim in any land-locked pool I can find these days, but I share my mum's anxiety now about waves. To be honest, I don't feel so much a water baby any more, but a water orphan. Since Suzy's accident ten years ago, if I swim, I swim alone – or at least, without my mum.' I turned over onto my back and stared up at the distant ceiling. 'That makes me sad.'

'I'm sorry,' said Hector. 'And there's me making flippant remarks about the backstories of swimmers.'

'It's okay, you weren't to know,' I said, plunging my head

briefly underwater to wash away the tears now filling my eyes. 'Anyway, you're right. It is interesting people-watching in swimming pools. I particularly like spotting unusual tattoos.'

Still in the rubber rings, we drifted on our backs for a bit, hands clasped like little otters, allowing the gentle current to propel us at its own pace.

'One last question, Sophie, then I'll shut up about it. Why does your mum choose to live in a house by the river if she's so scared of water?'

A sudden silence signalled that the wave cycle had finished, and people began to flock over to the rapid river in anticipation of that machine being turned on.

Hector put his feet on the floor and began to walk alongside me, one hand on my rubber ring, as I continued to paddle my feet.

'I feel like I'm taking my pet fish for a walk,' he remarked, making me laugh before I could answer his question.

'They bought the old hotel before Suzy died, so being close to water wasn't an issue then. The building was very run down, so it was a cheap way for them to acquire such a big house in a prime location. Oh, and because Dad fancied the fishing. Not that he fishes in the river these days, as Mum worries about him being swept away, especially if he goes out after a drink. Same with his hillwalking. But Mum wanted to stay in Scotland. This is home now. Plus, she thinks it's the best place to teach and study Gaelic. She's won quite a few research grants since she's been working here.'

'I'm glad her accident hasn't stopped you swimming. I can see you're a very good swimmer.' He paused to run his eyes slowly down my body as if wondering how I did it. Somehow the water began to feel warmer. 'Although I have heard that it's the strongest swimmers who drown.'

'So you're safe, then.' I wanted to tease him to lift our mood. Our first full day in Scotland together was turning out to be rather gloomy. 'Come on then, fish face, let's have a shot on the chutes. That's Scottish for having a turn on the slides, you great Sassenach.'

I threw off my rubber ring and launched myself into a rapid crawl towards the poolside.

18

DOWNWARD SPIRAL

We stood in front of the trio of long plastic tunnels in different shades of aquamarine that dominated the corner of the hall, each with a constant stream of water running down it and discharging into a small landing pool at ground level for every slide.

'Which slide do you recommend?' he asked, frowning.

I considered. 'Well, the straightest one is like a death slide, with a sheer drop. The other straight one has a gentler slope, which means you don't go quite as fast, so you don't get quite as much of an adrenaline rush.'

At that moment, there was an enormous splash as a grown man landed, gasping, at the foot of the death slide. It wasn't clear whether he'd enjoyed it.

'And the third slide?'

I grabbed his hand and dragged him towards it.

'Oh, that's my favourite. It's by far the most interesting and the best fun, and it lasts a lot longer than the others too – so more time in the pool in proportion to the time spent climbing the stairs and queuing. Come on, let's grab some rubber rings and go down it.'

I led him towards a pile of rubber rings, much bigger and stronger than the ones in the rapid river, as bright yellow as a bath-time duck, and with grab-handles at the sides.

'Oh good, more life preservers,' said Hector, sounding more cheerful. We grabbed one each. 'This is my kind of swimming.'

'This feature's called the Spiral,' I explained, as we began to climb the four flights of stairs to its starting point at ceiling height. I pointed to the height chart on the wall as we passed it halfway up. 'Don't worry, as long as you're more than a metre high, you'll be safe.'

He gave a sheepish grin.

'I'll go first to show you how it's done,' I said when we reached the top. 'Just do what I do a few seconds after I've gone down.'

I lobbed my rubber ring into the horizontal blue plastic channel at the start of the slide, sat down in it, gripped the grab-handles, and kicked myself off. The constant stream of water pumped down the slide oiled the way for me, and I sped, giggling, through the curves of the first tunnel before landing with a big splash in the first of the three pools that made up this feature, a separate tunnel between each one. The water shooting out of the end of the tunnel churned the little pool's waters into a whirlpool, sending me and my rubber ring travelling round the edge while I waited for Hector to emerge from the tunnel behind me.

After about a minute, he arrived with an even bigger splash than me, eyes screwed tight shut, shoulders hunched. For the sake of his dignity, I suppressed a smile.

Clearly disorientated, he opened his eyes and gazed about

him, smiling only when he saw me. The current dragged him in my wake.

'Make the most of this pool because it's the most relaxing of the three,' I advised him. 'The next two have showers at their centre that drench you with cold water if you're not quick enough to dodge them. Some people like to go under them on purpose or push each other in their path for fun.'

The current propelled us towards the tunnel that would bring us to the second little pool. Hector bobbed about helplessly, out of control.

'Push yourself off from the side and into the tunnel,' I told him. 'Like this.'

I cast my head back, crossed my arms across my chest, kept my legs tight together and my toes pointed. Then I lay back to increase my speed as I went.

Splashing down into the next pool, I ducked beneath the surface to avoid the icy jet of water at its centre, then emerged at the far side to wait for the tunnel to spit Hector out behind me. Suddenly he crashed into view, bumping his rubber ring so hard against mine that his rebounded, taking him right into the path of the chilly waterfall. He emerged, blinking and gasping, at the far side of the pool.

'My goodness, is that a storm drain? Whose mad idea was it to put that there?'

I laughed. 'It's given you an instant makeover, Hector, from merman to drowned rat!'

He wiped his hand across his face and shook his dripping, limp curls.

'Okay, let's get this over with. Down to the next one and out. I think the rapid river's more my style, to be honest.'

I launched my rubber ring into the next tunnel and slid down after it, landing in the third pool, where a queue of people was waiting to go down the final chute to the landing pool at ground level. I sat down, the water up to my chin, to await Hector's descent. I thought it better not to leave without him.

I waited and waited, but there was no sign of Hector. I was just at the point of wondering whether he had somehow managed to overtake me and already reached the exit point when he shot into view. Unsteadily, he got to his feet and waded past me to join the queue for the last tunnel. He seemed in a hurry to move on and get the experience over with.

'If you chuck your rubber ring down first, you'll have a more dignified landing at the bottom, and it's easier to set off before the next person lands behind you. Watch me, I'll show you.'

Moments later, I was climbing out of the landing pool onto the tiled surround, the bubbles from the chute flow still gushing round my feet and surging across the floor into the rapid river. I stretched and wrung out my hair, smoothed it back over my shoulders and waited to welcome my bedraggled merman.

And waited and waited, unable to see him due to the high blue plastic wall enclosing the final pool. I cupped my hands round my mouth to shout to him.

'Come on, Hector, just throw your ring down first and slide down after it. This last bit's easy-peasy.'

I knew he wouldn't hear me over the rushing waters, but I wanted to try to help him. I was feeling bad now for not being more sympathetic about his obvious nervousness of the Spiral. Perhaps he'd never been on anything like it before. I wondered what else I didn't know about Hector.

I was starting to be seriously worried that he might have knocked himself out with an awkward descent or passed out from a delayed reaction to his fall in the bookshop. Might he even be in the process of drowning? I was just about to ask the lifeguard at ground level to check the safety camera, when

Hector sailed down the exit slide in his doughnut, facing backwards. He fell over sideways, and out of the exit pool, landing on his hands and knees on the poolside with a bump. Unfazed by Hector's undignified exit, a scrawny teenager grabbed Hector's discarded rubber ring and scampered off towards the stairs.

As Hector stood up, his face was as dark as a thundercloud.

'I don't think that's very funny, Sophie, holding me under the deluge in the last pool like that.'

I took a step back. 'What? What do you mean? I never touched you. I was way ahead of you. Didn't you see me go down the last slide?'

He frowned as he realised his mistake. 'Yes, but for a moment I wondered if you'd dashed down the rest of the feature really quickly and gone round again. Now I realise you couldn't have done that quite that fast, but couldn't think who else would hold me under. But if it wasn't you, who was it?'

As we turned to check the exit pool for the latest arrival, a scrawny elderly lady in a stripey swimsuit climbed out of it.

'Well, unless she's got superpowers, I don't think she can have been your assailant.'

I stepped back to let her go by.

'Come on, Hector, we're creating a logjam. Unless you want to go down another slide, let's go back to the fun pool and play swimming-costume snap. Or sit in the Jacuzzi and see who can spot the best tattoo. There's always a fine selection in swimming pools. My favourites are the ones with a name crossed out. I always want to ask the story behind it. I saw a guy earlier with a treasure chest on his forearm. Do you think he was a pirate on his day off?'

He relaxed a little. 'You're a true writer, sweetheart. Real writers never stop working. They're always picking up material wherever they go.' He slipped his arm round my waist as we dripped a trail back to the pool.

'Maybe Hermione Minty's next romantic novel should be set at a leisure centre,' I suggested. 'Look, there's a storyline for you. That couple who were all over each other in the pool earlier are just going into the private shower room, and they haven't taken any shampoo, shower gel or towels. Do you think they're having a secret fling?'

Hector turned to follow where I was pointing, smiling for the first time since we'd entered the pool. 'Now there's an idea.'

Finally, he began to relax. We enjoyed three more circuits of the rapid river, waded through the big hole in the wall that led to the open-air paddling pool shaped like a thistle, and basked for ages in the Jacuzzi, which Hector declared to be his favourite feature of all. Then, all too soon for me, a distorted announcement over the tannoy told us it was the time for all swimmers with red wristbands to leave the pool.

As we approached our lockers, Hector clutched his wrist.

'Hang on, I've just realised I've lost the wristband with my locker key on it.'

I shook my head in disbelief. 'How could that have happened? Those wristbands are such a tight fit. They can't exactly fall off.' I took his left hand in mine. 'It was this arm you put it on, wasn't it?'

'Yes.'

'Well, you may not have your key, but you've got the makings of a fine bruise where your key used to be.'

He held up his arm to inspect the new dark mark.

'My goodness, you're right. Ouch!'

We turned down the row our lockers were in to find one of them wide open. Hector gave an anguished cry as he reached into the very back of it.

'Oh no, now all my clothes have gone. And your mum's book, too. It was in my jacket pocket, and my jacket's not there.'

'No, silly, you're looking in my locker, not yours. Look, it's got my clothes in it. All your stuff will be in the locker next to it, and that one's still locked.'

'But it was my key that went missing. This must be my locker.'

I slipped off the yellow wristband and held up its key to show him.

'So the one I was wearing must be your key. Look, it matches the number on the locked locker. But hang on. Don't you remember? Just after we changed into our swimsuits, I dropped my wristband on the floor, and you kindly picked it up for me. You must have inadvertently given me yours and put mine on your wrist. Then your wristband must have come off in the pool, and whoever picked it up came back here and opened my locker.'

I pulled my tote bag out and rummaged inside it.

'Fortunately, they don't seem to have taken anything. My phone and my purse are still there.'

Hector was still clutching his left wrist. 'That's not to say no damage has been done.'

He lifted his fingers to reveal the dark mark that had begun to form around his wrist.

I bit my lip. 'You poor thing, Hector, you are really going through the wars today. We'd better mention it to the staff on the way out.' For a moment I considered asking them also to check their video footage to see if someone really had held him underwater, as he believed. But I didn't want to embarrass him. His ego had already suffered enough. 'Now, let's get showered and changed. Here, take your key so you can get your stuff.'

I slipped it off my wrist and pressed it into his hand.

After we'd changed back into our clothes, we reported the loss of his key to the centre manager at reception. She was sympathetic, but as perplexed as we were.

'I'm sorry we didn't spot anything amiss,' she said. 'But if a person opened the locker with a key, we'd have thought nothing of it. That's not suspicious. That's how the system is meant to work. But if nothing was taken, maybe it was just an honest mistake. Or perhaps you just forgot to lock it in your excitement to get into the pool. Still, I can see you're upset about it, so let's make amends.' She fished underneath the desk for a moment and pulled out a laminated voucher the size of a business card. 'Here, enjoy a free swim on us by way of compensation. Haste ye back now.'

'Thank you very much. That's very kind. We will.'

'Will we?' Hector sounded doubtful.

I slipped the voucher into my purse, and we turned to go, zipping up our cagoules against the rain.

19

IN THE GARDEN

'Don't mention our little problem at the swimming pool to Mum,' I said to Hector as we crossed the Infirmary Bridge, heading back to my parents' house in time for tea. 'Nor your fall at McNab's. She worries too much about her family's safety without us fuelling her anxiety.'

'Are you sure this bridge is safe?' Hector moved to the far right to grasp the handrail. If he had learned his lesson from his fall in the bookshop, his caution was now misplaced.

'Yes, it's entirely safe, don't worry.' I moved across to slip my arm round his waist. 'The bridge has always been like this, but you're not the first tourist to be freaked out by the way it shakes underfoot when crossing it for the first time. It still terrifies Mum, but then she is so easily terrified since Suzy's accident.'

I stamped my feet a couple of times to make it tremble even more. The familiar juddering sound resonated across the Ness.

'I suppose the Scots are trustworthy engineers,' he conceded as we reached the highest point. 'All those Stevensons, with their lighthouses and railways.'

'Not to mention Thomas Telford,' I added. 'We've him to thank for the Caledonian Canal.'

Just then a couple of teenagers on bikes came tearing towards us, shouting and laughing, and making the bridge shake even more in the few seconds it took them to whizz across it.

I looked at Hector out of the corner of my eye. He wasn't usually the anxious type, but his brace of accidents today seemed to have really unnerved him. When he caught me watching him, he gave me an embarrassed smile, and tightened his arm around my shoulders.

When we reached the far bank, we followed the riverside footpath to the high wooden gate that led to my mum and dad's back garden. I raised the latch and pushed the gate open. The garden was long and wide, lined with native trees and flower beds filled with low-maintenance shrubs. A number of ancient wooden park benches were dotted about the garden, left over from the days when the house had been a hotel. There was one bench for each of the eight bedrooms, in the unlikely event that all the hotel guests, even during full occupancy, would all sit in the garden at once. I gravitated towards my favourite bench beneath a squat, sturdy oak. The kitchen light was on. Mum must have been home already and was very likely putting our dinner on. She was a very good cook, especially when she used local Highland ingredients.

Hector laid his arm around my shoulders, and I snuggled up beside him, taking care not to press too hard in case I touched any of his growing collection of bruises.

'So how are you feeling now, Hector?' As I spoke, I watched him.

He touched a hand to his waist.

'To be honest, my back hurts a bit since I fell down the stairs, but I'm fine, really. Just a bit shaken, I suppose. I don't think I was ever in real danger in the swimming pool, but I was startled when whoever it was ducked me. From their strength, I'm guessing it was a man. He used both hands, one on the top of my head, the other on my left shoulder.' He rubbed his left shoulder thoughtfully. 'They weren't just larking about. It wasn't a playful or flirtatious gesture. There was anger in it.'

I squeezed his hand in sympathy.

'The same breed of aggression that might be present in someone who'd push a person down a flight of stairs?'

Hector's eyes widened.

'Surely not. That would be too much of a coincidence. Do you really think both acts were by the same person?'

I moved a little closer to him, as much for my comfort as for his. I was glad he was beginning to agree with me that his fall in McNab's might have been no accident, even though I didn't want to believe that myself.

'Anyone at McNab's might easily have deduced we were going swimming, because when we arrived at the changing area, I noticed my bikini top was hanging over the edge of my bag, protruding from the rolled-up towel. But, as it was bone dry, as was our hair, it was clear we'd not been to the pool yet. It was hardly rocket science to work out that was where we'd go next – as indeed Mr McNab did.'

'But we didn't go straight there, did we? We went to the cathedral.'

I huffed. 'That's such an easy place for anyone to hide, though. Your assailant could have lurked anywhere in the big shadowy building while we were looking around. If he lingered in the pews to watch us, all he needed to do to disguise himself if we turned in his direction was to drop to his knees and cover his face with his hands as if in prayer.'

'Surely you don't think he was planning to attack me in the

cathedral? Even though there were a lot of tourists about, it was so quiet, he couldn't have got away with even the stealthiest assault.'

'No, but he might have been tailing us, just to make sure we really were going to the swimming pool next.'

'Do you think he was spying on us in the coffee shop afterwards too?' asked Hector. 'It was quite small, with only a handful of tables. It would have been much harder for someone to hide there.'

I considered it for a moment.

'No, if I were him, I'd have bypassed the coffee shop to get a head start over us at the leisure centre. He could have waited in the pool, lurking anywhere in the waters until we arrived. We'd be easy to spot, and in case he didn't recognise me without my clothes on, he would have known what colour bikini to look for as he had already seen the top sticking out of my bag.'

Hector wagged his forefinger.

'No, he'd have waited for us to get there so that he'd be given the same colour wristband as ours. Otherwise, if we'd been a long time over our coffee, his time in the pool might have been over before we even entered the water.'

I thought about our stroll from the coffee shop to the pool.

'There were plenty of places he could have hidden along the way too. All those bushes surrounding the mini golf course or behind the cars parked at the ice hockey centre. There are quite a lot of hedges in the leisure centre's landscaped gardens surrounding the swimming pool complex, and there are some trees around the shinty field that are big enough to conceal a person.'

Hector nodded.

'Yes, I bet that's what he did. He followed us into the waters. He got into the pool after we did and followed us round.' He paled. 'Another easy place to hide. If he thought we might spot him, he could have just taken a deep breath and submerged himself to avoid detection.'

I exhaled through pursed lips.

'You're right. But what we haven't worked out is why on earth would anyone bother to follow us? Why push you down the stairs? Why duck you? If he was just an opportunistic thief, there were surely much easier pickings all around him. I bet I wasn't the only one to leave my bag on the floor in McNab's while browsing the bookshelves. That's something you can't do one-handed, so unless you've got a cross body bag or a backpack, you'd have to put your bag down. Plus, the browser's attention is distracted. It would be easy for a seasoned thief to pinch my purse or my phone or even my whole tote bag while I was engrossed in an interesting book. But who would push someone downstairs to distract him from being pickpocketed? That's hardly the work of a master criminal.'

'And if theft was their motivation, why didn't they take anything from your locker when they were able to?'

'Perhaps they didn't have time. They might have seen us coming or realised one of the staff was watching them and had to run for it before they could take anything.'

'No, they had plenty of time after my wristband – I mean, your wristband – was stolen. They'd have had plenty of time to pick and choose what they fancied from your locker.'

'Yes, we were ages in the pool after we'd finished on the Spiral.'

'That was the best bit at the end, sitting in the Jacuzzi, all safe and cosy.'

The wistful note in his voice made me stare at him in surprise and sudden realisation.

'Hector,' I said slowly. 'Am I right in thinking you can't swim?'

He put his elbows on his knees and buried his face in his hands.

'Blast! You've rumbled me, sweetheart, and I thought I'd got away with it. I'm sorry.' His words were muffled by his palms. 'I didn't realise until we came up here how important swimming was to you and your mum, and I didn't want to look stupid in front of either of you by admitting I was a non-swimmer.'

I laid a comforting hand on his shoulder. 'Don't be daft, Hector, we all have an Achilles heel.' I'd been reading Greek mythology since my Ithaca trip.

'Yes, and look what happened to Achilles!'

I patted his back.

'Anyway, I'd never have thought any less of you for that, and nor would Mum. I'm sure that there are plenty of things you can do that I can't. Driving, for instance. And writing so many successful romantic novels. You don't think any less of me because I can't drive, do you?'

Hector lifted his head from his hands and raised his eyebrows in surprise. 'No, of course not. Though I'd be very happy if you did learn to drive. Next time we come up here, or go elsewhere on holiday, it would be great to be able to share the driving.'

Just then the back door opened, and my dad emerged bearing two mugs of tea.

'Hello, you two. Had a good day?'

When he reached us, he handed us each a mug and bent to kiss the top of my head. I beamed, perhaps a little too much, and he eyed me suspiciously.

'Yes, thanks, Dad. Action-packed. McNab's, the cathedral, the cathedral's café and a lovely swim at the corporation pool. How about you?'

As he sat down on the nearest bench and began to tell us about his day, I slipped my hand into Hector's and stroked it with my other hand to show him I still thought the world of him. Rather than let go of his hand, I let my tea get cold.

20

AT THE PIANO

'Mr McNab took a look at your book for us today, Mum. You left it behind when you went to work this morning, so Hector took it in to show him when we went into town.'

Mum had just sat down to join us at the table after setting a dish of rich, dark-brown venison casserole beside a bowl of mashed potatoes and another of green beans. I spooned some of each onto my plate, admiring the contrast of the gleaming dark gravy against the matte cloud of mash.

'Thank you, darling. So did he have anything interesting to say about it?'

I motioned to Hector to help himself to food, which he did with alacrity. Swimming always makes you hungry, apparently even if you can't actually swim.

'I'm afraid it's not valuable in financial terms,' I explained. 'It's not rare. Mr McNab had a lot of other copies on his shelves in various editions and states of repair, but none were very expensive. But he said the inscription might make it valuable as a piece of social history. He agreed with your translation of the inscription as a massive moralising rant by the giver to the recipient, who seems to share his name. He says it's an improving kind of book, full of poems telling the reader how to lead a godly, sober life. The inscription echoes its sentiments in a terser, angrier format.'

Dad laughed.

'No wonder the recipient gave it away. I'm guessing he didn't take kindly to the message, and that it didn't magically transform him into the clean-living, upright citizen that the giver hoped for. I bet he never even read it.'

Mum took her turn at the casserole.

'It does rather highlight the nature of Hebridean morals, until recent times, at least. Not that they were ever averse to a wee dram.' She looked sideways at my father through narrowed eyes. 'But they certainly went on keeping the Sabbath long after most people gave up on the mainland. Until quite recently, they even used to lock up the swings in the children's playparks on Sundays.'

She set down the serving spoon and picked up the carafe of water to fill her glass.

'Excellent water around here, by the way, Hector.' She raised her glass to him. 'So soft and pure, especially compared to the hard limey stuff in the Cotswolds. You never have to worry about your kettle scaling up around here.'

Dad poured dark-red wine into my glass, Hector's and his own without looking at Mum.

'I hope you're still pleased with the book,' Hector added. 'I confess I only paid a pound for it at a car boot sale. To my mind, second-hand books aren't like gemstones or stocks and shares. Their true value can be in the curiosity factor rather than the resale value.'

I wondered how he'd reconcile that philosophy with profitable trading when he opened his second-hand department. To his obvious relief, Mum agreed.

'Yes, and I think this little book is sufficiently interesting to justify its being shared with a wider audience and kept for posterity.'

Hector sat up straighter, somehow taller for her praise.

'You mean like putting it in a museum, Mum?' I put in. 'I was planning to take Hector to the City Museum at some point this week, so we could take it with us if you like.'

Mum took a sip of water.

'That wouldn't be the best place for it. Their displays are mostly to do with ancient and natural history rather than highland and island life.'

'How about the Highland Archive Centre on the road to Whin Park?' suggested Dad.

It was an easy, pleasant walk from my parents' house.

'Ooh, yes. I was planning to take him to Whin Park too.'

Dad gave me an affectionate smile. 'Never too old for the miniature railway, eh, love?'

I had many fond memories of riding around Whin Park with Dad on the little model train and taking rowing boats and pedalos out onto the lake.

'Actually, I was thinking it might make a nice addition to one of the room settings in the old cottages at the Highland Outdoor Heritage Museum, where it would be seen by more people,' said Mum. 'Dad and I are both free on Friday. Why don't we make a family outing of it and all go together? They're adding new exhibits all the time, and I haven't been for a year or two. It would be good to catch up with the archivists too. I know a couple of them socially.'

'Oh yes,' I cried. 'I hadn't planned to take Hector there this week, as it would mean more driving, but if we all went, you or dad could drive and give him a break.'

'I'm trying to encourage Sophie to learn to drive,' added Hector. 'Not that I mind driving her anywhere.'

Dad nodded approval. 'About time too, Sophie.'

When we'd finished our meal, we adjourned to the snug. As Mum went to make coffee, Dad slipped the rest of the bottle of wine under his armchair, no doubt planning to polish it off surreptitiously by himself.

Hector strode over to the piano and lifted the lid. 'May I?'

'Help yourself,' said Dad, settling back in his armchair. 'It will be good to hear it played again. It used to belong to the hotel, and Sophie learned to play on it. It barely gets touched these days with Sophie being away, but we've had it tuned regularly over the years to maintain its condition.'

Hector's brow furrowed in concentration as he played Beethoven's 'Für Elise' – every school child's party piece, although I've never understood why. It's too easy to sound wooden and heartless while concentrating on hitting the right notes, massacring its flowing melody. Hector's rendition was technically correct but devoid of emotion, the pianist's equivalent of an AI robot singing, *'Je ne regrette rien'*. Considering how fond Hector was of music – he was always playing it in the shop, and he delighted in picking a tune to suit each customer – the indifference of his performance startled me.

Oblivious of my opinion, Hector rose, smiling, from the piano stool.

'It would be impossible not to play well on such a beautiful instrument,' he declared.

'Dad, I think it's overdue to be tuned,' I said, to avoid the need to praise his performance.

Dad pulled his phone from his trouser pocket to search for the piano tuner's contact details.

'Your turn now, love,' he said, as he began to type him a text message.

Hector patted the velvet-topped piano stool to encourage me.

'Oh, I don't know. Perhaps I'd better go and help Mum in the kitchen.'

The rattle of a tray full of cups just outside the door told me this excuse wouldn't work. Hector went to open the door for her as Dad looked up from his phone.

'Go on, Sophie. Show Hector what you can do. Play me my favourite, would you?'

'Oh yes, please, dear, that would be nice,' added Mum, setting the tray on the coffee table.

Reluctant as I was to show Hector up in front of them, I could hardly refuse. I flipped open the piano stool to retrieve a thick music book that lived in the little cubbyhole beneath the seat.

'More Beethoven, I'm afraid,' I said to Hector, then felt stupid in case he thought I was belittling the great composer. I sat down on the piano stool, opened the book at Piano Concerto No. 32, placed it on the music stand and twiddled the little brass levers to secure it in place. As Hector crossed the room to the sofa, I began to play.

As the final chord faded and I laid my tingling hands in my lap, there was a brief silence before my dad broke into enthusiastic applause.

'Well done, dear,' said Mum. 'A little rusty, perhaps, but lovely to hear, all the same. What a shame there's no space even for an upright in May's cottage.'

I returned the music book to the piano stool, stood up and

stretched my back, raising my arms over my head. I'd used muscles that had lain dormant for too long.

Hector's eyes were glazed. 'Lucy Honeychurch,' he murmured, before looking up to answer my question. 'That was amazing. Like Lucy Honeychurch in *A Room with a View*.'

Dad coughed. 'So, are you descended from the Black Isle Munros, Hector? There's a lot of them in Cromarty, at its far end.'

Hector blinked, his mind apparently still on Lucy Honeychurch. Perhaps he was wondering whether I saw him more as George Emerson or Cecil Vyse.

'The Black Isle?' he echoed. 'No, sorry. Is that the same as in the Tintin book, *The Black Island*? I've never been there.'

Dad raised his eyebrows in mild scorn. 'Well, you're pretty close to the real Black Isle now, which isn't an island at all, but a peninsula. It's just across the bridge from Inverness.'

'Not one of the little bridges that span the River Ness,' I put in, 'but the big one, the Kessock Bridge, that carries the A9 north from Inverness.'

Hector shook his head apologetically.

'Sorry to disappoint you, but my family are all from south of the border, at least as far as I know. I suppose the name might trace back to Scottish ancestry at some point on my father's side.'

'But your parents gave you a Scottish first name,' said my dad, as if he thought persisting might turn Hector irretrievably Scottish.

'Ha! That's rich, Dad! Your name's Gordon and Mum's is Shona, but that doesn't make either of you any more Scottish than Hector.'

As Dad raised his hand authoritatively, I had a glimpse of him in his role as a lecturer at the university.

'Ah, but Sayers is as English as they come. A diminutive of the occupational name of Sawyer, Hector, dating back further than the Domesday Book. I was named Gordon after a distant Scottish relative who my parents thought might remember me in his will. He didn't, by the way. And Mum's parents just liked the name Shona.'

Hector shifted in his seat.

'Actually, I was named after the ancient Greek Hector and my twin brother after Horace. I don't think Scotland was on my parents' mind at all. They were more interested in the classics.'

Dad's face fell.

'Do you even know about the Munros? The mountains, I mean, not the Black Isle folk.'

Hector glanced at me for moral support.

'Don't worry, Dad, I've told him all about them. I've told him about your passion for climbing them too. He knows about Munro baggers who want to collect them all. He even said he'd like to go up one of the hills with you one day, didn't you, Hector?'

He hadn't, but I thought saying so might help Hector bond with Dad.

Dad beamed, rubbing his hands together in anticipation.

'Excellent. How about we tackle the Cuillins together? They're on Skye. I love Skye.'

'The Cuillins?' Mum's eyes widened in horror as she looked from Dad to me and back again. 'A bit far to go for a day trip,' she faltered. 'Sophie and Hector won't have time to do that this week, dear.'

Dad shrugged.

'Got to do it sometime if I'm to bag the lot before I get too old for it.'

'A trip to Skye would be lovely,' I said evenly, although I

remembered vividly our disastrous last trip there, just before I'd left home for university. Dad had lost his way on the hill after taking a hip flask of Scotch with him and taking a wrong turning. He had had to call Mountain Rescue to bring him down safely. He was extremely lucky that he managed to get a signal on his phone to report his accident. The topography and the magnetic fields of the Cuillins make mobiles almost useless up there.

Meanwhile, Mum and I, oblivious to his unfolding disaster, had taken a picnic to an idyllic natural water feature at the foot of the hills, where unfortunately Mum had had a flashback to Suzy's drowning and ended up sobbing by the water's edge. By the end of the day, I was the only one of the three of us with all my wits about me. Goodness knows how Mum drove us home – Dad couldn't as he'd still have been over the limit. That was yet another occasion that I regretted being unable to drive.

'Hector, it's a beautiful, clear evening,' I said, getting up from the piano stool at last. 'How about a post-dinner stroll on Ness Islands?'

'Ness Islands?' repeated Hector. 'Do ferries run there this time of night?'

Mum, Dad, and I were all glad of a reason to laugh, to dispel the awkwardness that had descended.

'No, silly, by a little footbridge just up the road. Don't you remember? I mentioned them to you yesterday, when we first arrived.'

Hector sighed with relief. He probably felt he'd had enough adventures for one day.

'I'll get our coats,' he offered, rising from his chair and heading for the hall.

As I closed the drawing room door behind me, I heard Mum lay into Dad about the now empty wine bottle beside his chair.

21

ON NESS ISLANDS

'So, what are they like to climb, these Cuillins?' asked Hector as we strolled down the back garden path towards the riverside walk.

I closed the gate behind us and slipped my hand into his.

'Don't worry, it's just hillwalking, really, not climbing with ropes and ice-picks and crampons. Not at this time of year, anyway. Provided you wear the right kit, especially proper walking boots, plan your journey, tell someone where you're going.' I hesitated, not wanting to put him off. I decided not to tell him that the Cuillins included of the most challenging terrain in Britain. 'Just stick with Dad and follow his instructions and you'll be fine. You never know, you might even enjoy it.'

More than the swimming at least, I thought, mentally crossing my fingers.

Hector released my hand so he could put his arm round my shoulders, and I slipped my arm about his waist.

'You're right about that, Sophie, which is why, the more I think about it, the more I think your interpretation of the incident in McNab's is correct. I may not be entirely confident in a swimming pool.' I suppressed a smile to spare his pride. 'But I am too steady on my feet to tumble down a flight of stairs without being given a helping hand. But who would push me, and why? It's not as if anyone knows me up here.'

'Whereas in Wendlebury, where everyone knows you, they're queuing up to push you down stairs.' I gave a hollow laugh. 'Perhaps you'd better reconsider your plans to install a second-hand department in your flat above the shop. You'd just be putting temptation in someone's way to shove you off the landing to your death.'

We turned onto the little wrought iron bridge to cross to Ness Islands, which, as ever, were looking magical, with tiny, coloured fairy lights twinkling in the trees. Hector eyed the pathway ahead of us, which was bordered by shadowy nooks among the trees and shrubs. The dark waters of the Ness rushed by on either side.

'Are you sure it's safe here after dark?' he asked.

'Yes, of course. Just as safe as it was walking in the dark to the barn for the village Halloween party last autumn. And there we didn't have the benefit of fairy lights to help us on our way.'

'Sorry, Sophie, I'm being a wimp. I guess I'm just slightly on edge after the strange accidents since we left Wendlebury.'

I fell silent. I still wasn't convinced that any of the series of events was an accident, least of all poor Alasdair's death. As for Hector, if someone was so intent on attacking him that they would push him down a flight of stairs in the middle of a busy shop and duck him underwater in a public pool while on camera, who knew just how murderous they might get under the cover of darkness, with only me as witness? Perhaps I shouldn't have brought him here.

Just then, the fairy lights flickered and cut out for a moment, making my heart pound before they came on again. I began to walk a little faster, and Hector stepped out to keep up with me.

'By the way, thanks for not mentioning those little incidents in McNab's and the swimming pool to Mum and Dad today,' I said, slipping my arm through his as we wound our way round the path towards the footbridge that led to the second island. Then I stopped abruptly, pointing! 'Ooh, look, the monster!'

Rather sweetly, Hector wrapped his arms protectively around me. I patted his hand comfortingly

'It's not a real one, silly,' I told him. 'Not *the* monster. Just a sculpture of one carved out of an old tree trunk. See?'

I pointed to a large, low log with a smiley face. Hector's laugh was a little high pitched.

'Oh yes, I knew that.' He cleared his throat, before changing the subject. 'But what I didn't know was how well you could play the piano. I wouldn't have touched it myself if I'd known how much better your performance would be.'

He took my hand as we set off again at a brisk pace, in perfect step with each other.

'I'd hardly call it a performance. I was only playing my dad's favourite.'

'Yes, but a very tricky favourite. How come I've never heard you play before?'

'I've no piano in my cottage, and you don't have one in your house. I think you'll find it's not possible to demonstrate my piano-playing prowess in the absence of a piano.'

We stopped at a fork in the path.

'Which way now?' asked Hector, looking about us.

I indicated the bridge that would take us to the far bank of the Ness and we began to head towards it.

'My parents have a piano in their bungalow in Clevedon,'

Hector continued. 'Why have you never played it when we've been visiting them?'

'It didn't occur to me. It would be a bit presumptuous.'

'Nonsense. Next time you must. No one ever plays it since Horace and I left home. My parents will be very impressed. They used to despair of Horace and me. We never practised between lessons. You know I love music, but that doesn't make me a musician, any more than enjoying watching football would make one a great player.'

I wrinkled my nose.

'I'm not that good. Only grade eight. I never took it any further after I left school, apart from teaching it to small children. When I was at university, it was an easy source of income. I got in touch with a few local primary schools who spread the word for me, and before long I had as many young students as I could fit in around my studies. I could choose my own hours, and it was better paid than working behind a bar or in a shop.'

'Or in a tearoom.' Hector sounded dejected as we stepped off the bridge onto the riverbank. I steered him to the right, so that we could circle back towards my parents' house.

I didn't reply. It was all right for him. He was the proprietor of the bookshop. Running the bookshop was his career, or rather one of his careers. The romantic novels he published under a pen name to supplement his income from the shop was a second successful career. Me, I was just a waitress who helped a few kids with their reading on the side, and whose only published writing was my monthly column, 'Travels with my Aunt's Garden', in Wendlebury's parish magazine. My first novel, a fictionalised memoir of my life in the village (working title: *Best Murder in Show*), was still very much a work-in-progress. Being a competent amateur pianist didn't count in the career stakes.

'Well, you didn't tell me you couldn't swim,' I blurted out, as if his omission might cancel out mine.

'That's hardly the same thing. Like I'm going to go out of my way to point out my faults.'

Desperately trying to think how to prevent this turning into an argument, I stared into the distance. The city lights twinkled in the distance, car headlights moving slowly across Ness Bridge, in the shadow of the floodlit castle.

So far our holiday was turning into a disaster, with one dead body, two possible assaults on my boyfriend, and my mum and dad at loggerheads over my dad's drinking, as usual.

'Well, at least my mum was pleased with the book you bought her,' I said at last, clutching at this one positive fact. 'Where's the book now, by the way?'

'At your folks' house. I put it back on the side table where your mum left it this morning, so I guess it'll stay there now till we take it to that museum she mentioned on Friday. The Highland Outdoor Heritage Museum, was it?'

'Yes, that'll be a nice day out.' I squeezed his hand. 'Just think, you'll be leaving your mark on Scotland if the book you bought ends up in a museum.'

'So far it feels more like Scotland's leaving its mark on me.'

He rubbed his back where he'd bruised it falling down the stairs earlier. Then, for no apparent reason, he slapped his palm against his neck.

'Ow!' he cried, aggrieved. 'What on earth was that?' He glanced around anxiously. 'A poisoned dart? Ow, now one's hit my cheek.'

He put his hand to his face.

'Oh, no!' I gazed up at a shaft of light from a streetlamp, spotting tiny black dots buzzing around us. 'Wretched midges! I thought their season would be over by now. Or else I'd have doused us in Skin-So-Soft before we came out.'

'Skin-So-Soft? What's that?'

'It's an Avon skincare product that for some reasons midges can't abide. The military up here use it by the bucketful. Now, quick, unless you've got a cigarette on you to light up and send them packing, the best thing to do is run for it. Either that or jump into the nearest body of water. They won't follow you into water.'

'You know I don't smoke,' he replied tersely.

I tugged his hand urgently, then let go so that we could run faster, unhindered by each other.

As we entered the rickety bridge, Hector gave a little shriek of alarm. It shook far more when you ran on it. Soon, we were hurtling up the garden path, before letting ourselves in at the kitchen door and slamming it behind us.

Just then, my dad strolled into the kitchen, heading for the coffee machine to find us flushed and breathless.

'Nice stroll, love?' He winked at me. 'That's what I like to see, the Highland air putting a bit of colour back into your cheeks.'

'That's one way of putting it,' I replied, slipping off my coat.

22

TARTAN DREAMS

Mum and Dad had allocated us one of the bedrooms that still bore the former hotel's full-on tartan look – carpet, curtains, bedspread, wallpaper.

'It must have been hell trying to line this lot up,' said Hector, running his hand appreciatively over a perfectly matched join on the wallpaper by the door.

I sat at the dressing table and began to take off my earrings.

'Did you get very badly bitten by those midges, Hector?'

He ran his fingertips cautiously over his forehead and cheeks, and delved beneath his collar.

'I can feel a few bites starting to itch now, but I suppose it could have been worse. How about you?'

He came over to stand behind me, stroking my hair as he watched me in the mirror. I opened a jar of moisturiser and began to massage a thin layer into my nose and cheeks.

'I got off Scot free.' Catching his eye in his reflection in the mirror, I forced a laugh at my bad joke. 'Funnily enough, they don't much go for me. I guess the midges round here prefer foreign food.'

He chuckled as he picked up a section of my hair from my crown and began to plait it. I suppose with his head of natural curls, my dead straight locks must hold a certain fascination for him, or at least novelty value.

'What are we going to do tomorrow? Should I wear body armour this time to guard against any further assaults on my person?'

I wasn't sure whether he was just trying to be funny, or whether he was starting to believe that someone might be after him.

'I'd have liked to take you to a Highland Games,' I replied, 'but the season's over.'

I was genuinely disappointed.

'Ha! That's a shame, with all the possibilities those would bring for further violence, what with all those beefy men tossing cabers about, and dancing the Highland Fling over crossed swords. Plus don't they tuck daggers into their long woollen socks, ready to stab at a moment's notice? No, thank you, Sophie!'

'They're not daggers, they're *sgian-dubhs*,' I corrected him testily. I loved Highland dress and all the associated traditions.

'Not to mention death by a thousand bagpipes,' he continued, cringing at the thought. Then he stepped back to admire his handiwork on my hair, before sitting down on the tartan bedspread.

'Seriously, though, Sophie, could it really be that someone has got it in for me up here? I mean who would even know me unless,' his eyes widened, 'there's some insanely jealous ex of yours lurking up here, waiting to finish me off and shove me in the Ness, clearing his way back to your heart.'

I rolled my eyes.

'You don't write romantic novels for nothing, do you?'

He gave me a lopsided grin as I swung round on the dressing table stool to face him.

'Hector, I can't imagine why anyone would attack you. Maybe I am overreacting. Just because you're usually sure-footed doesn't make you immune to occasionally slipping on a shiny spiral staircase. You heard what Mr McNab said about Morag's zeal for floor polish. Perhaps no one ducked you in the pool, either. You just had a panic attack because you weren't comfortable in that fast-flowing whirlpool. I'm sorry, I would never have taken you in there if I'd known you couldn't swim.'

His face fell.

'Anyway, if it makes you feel better, remember I can't drive, and that's a lot worse than being unable to swim, don't you think?'

He smiled at last and grabbed my hands, pulling me off the stool and onto the bed.

'Yes, you're useless, Sophie. Now come here and show me something you can do.'

I lay back and he began to kiss me.

23

LOCH NESS MONSTROSITY

'Good lord, did you know there was a man found murdered at Gretna Green on the day you came up here?

Dad lowered the newspaper to peer at us across the breakfast table. He resumed reading for a moment.

'A bookseller too, from Wigtown. I wonder what he did to upset his attacker?'

'He was—' I was about to say he had seemed a perfectly amenable man and that it must have been an unprovoked attack, but I stopped myself just in time. It would seem very odd if they discovered only now that we'd known all about it – had been witnesses, even – and hadn't thought to mention it when we had arrived. I imagined Dad asking us how the journey had been and replying, 'Oh, fine, just the one dead bookseller along the way.'

Hector came to my rescue.

'I gather Wigtown is Scotland's equivalent of Hay-on-Wye, a mecca of second-hand bookshops.'

I was grateful to him for steering us back on to safer ground.

'Hector's going to be opening a second-hand department when we get back. Hector, tell Dad your plans.'

Mum set a rack of toast and a dish of hot potato scones on the table.

'Well, you've an eye for it if you can spot a historically interesting book like the one you kindly brought me, even in a foreign language,' she said, setting the items on the table.

I helped myself to a potato scone and began to butter it. The hot surface made the butter melt faster than I could spread it.

'The new department will be in his spare bedroom in his flat above the shop, so he'll lose a bit of privacy. But he's very tidy and quite minimalist, so it should be fine.'

'The antidote to May's cottage, then,' Mum teased me.

'Sophie's cottage now, love,' Dad corrected her.

'Still just as cluttered, though,' I confessed. 'But that's how I like it.'

'Opposites attract, eh, love?' said Dad, looking at Mum, who didn't meet his gaze.

'So, what are you two up to today?' she asked, topping up Hector's coffee cup from the cafetiere.

'There's still a week before the Loch Ness cruises stop for the season,' Dad suggested. He ignored Mum's disapproving look. 'That's always nice for anyone who's never been on one before.'

'Always nice for someone who has, too,' I declared. 'For this someone, anyway.'

A shadow passed across Mum's face.

'Just don't go out on deck, darling, please. It's going to be chilly and wet this morning. You don't want to catch cold and spoil your holiday. You can borrow our waxed jackets to keep you warm and dry.'

* * *

As we shuffled forward in the queue at Dochgarroch Lock south of the city, the drizzle was turning heavier. We'd driven there in the Land Rover, but I was glad we'd borrowed Mum and Dad's green waxed jackets, even if they did make us look middle-aged, like half the rest of the passengers. Hector eyed at the small motor cruiser we were shortly to board.

'What's your mum got against travelling on deck? Surely, she doesn't believe that old wives' tale that getting cold gives you a cold?'

I took my tote bag off my shoulder and hugged it to my chest to stop the doddery old lady behind from bumping against it every time she took a too-eager step forward. From her inability to queue nicely, I guessed she was a foreign tourist.

'I'm afraid it's still her fear of drowning. If she thought I was going to be standing on deck, she'd be worrying all day that I'd fall over the edge and drown.'

Hector slipped his satchel to his other side so that he could put his arm around my shoulders without it coming between us.

'But as we have already established, you're a strong swimmer. Surely, you'd be all right even if you did fall overboard? She doesn't think you'd get eaten by the fabled monster, does she? I mean, it's only a lake. It's not like it's the open sea.'

I glanced around us, hoping no one had overheard.

'Not only is it a loch, not a lake, but it's the largest body of fresh water in the British Isles and contains more water than all the others put together.'

Hector frowned.

'It doesn't look big enough for that. Not unless it's miles deep.'

'Oh, it's deep, all right. Twice as deep as the North Sea in places. But this is only the start of it. It's still quite narrow here. Once we're in the boat and on our way, you'll see how much the loch broadens out in front of us. It's so vast, that out in the middle, in bad weather, it can get really rough and dangerous, with waves and everything. Anyway, whatever the weather we'll be fine on this boat. It doesn't go far out into the loch, only travelling as far as Castle Urquhart, and we keep quite close to the shore.'

Turning the final corner in the queue, we presented our tickets to the crew member on the gangplank. We trudged down onto the deck, and I preceded Hector down the steps into the covered lounge below, where I nabbed the last free double window seat.

'We'll be a lot warmer below deck anyway,' I told him as we settled down and undid our waxed jackets. 'It gets surprisingly cold up on top with the wind coming across the loch.'

As the boat chugged away from the harbourside, we sat back, listening to the commentary, craning our necks to view the famous osprey nests in the treetops as we passed them by, before the captain began milking the Loch Ness Monster myth for all it was worth.

Before long, the magnificent ruin of Castle Urquhart came into view to our right, looking all the more mysterious through the condensation on the windows, caused by the moisture evaporating from the passengers' damp coats.

Hector rummaged in his satchel for his phone.

'I'll just nip up top to take a photo, Sophie,' he said. 'I'll never get a clear image through those steamed-up windows. I want to send a picture of Loch Ness to my mum and dad.'

I watched Hector head up the stairs. Doubtless he wouldn't miss the opportunity to show his twin brother Horace, either, that he wasn't the only adventurous one. How funny it would be if Hector spotted the Loch Ness Monster while he was up here, I mused. A real-life monster would trump Horace's tales of the crocodiles he wrestles in his work as an Australian Outback tour guide. I sometimes wondered if Horace's tales of his bravado were true, or whether he just liked to frighten their mum.

Just then there came a scream, as a dark figure plummeted past the window into the waters below. A split second after a loud splash, I realised the figure was wearing a green waxed jacket just like my dad's.

24

THE MISSING SATCHEL

I let out a shriek and rushed up the stairs, holding on to both handrails to get up there as fast as I could. Just as well I did, as it braced me against a massive jolt, caused by the captain putting the ship into reverse.

As I gained the deck, I crashed right into Hector, who was just about to descend the steps, dry as a desert. I threw myself into his arms and gave him the fiercest hug of my life.

'So, it wasn't you who fell from the deck, Oh, thank goodness!'

He hugged me back.

'Did you see him jump?' I whispered. 'Or was he pushed?'

'Let's go below,' he said quietly, turning me round, and I gladly retreated down the steps.

There was a loud buzz of chatter all around us as the other passengers compared notes on what they thought they'd seen and their theories on survival rates in the murky depths of Loch Ness. Then a crackle over the tannoy heralded an official announcement.

'Ladies and gentlemen, boys and girls, this is your captain

speaking. Thank you for your calm.' Perhaps he hoped the power of suggestion would have the desired effect on the agitated crowd. 'I'm pleased to report the gentleman who unfortunately took an unexpected dip in the loch has been successfully recovered and brought back on deck. Our first-aider is now attending to him, and, as a precaution, an ambulance is on its way to meet him when we dock. As we are still closer to our point of departure than to Castle Urquhart, we will return immediately to our point of embarkation to ensure a speedier transition to hospital. You will of course receive a refund or a ticket for a later journey to make amends for any inconvenience caused by this unprecedented mishap. In the meantime, anyone who has seen the gentleman's bag, a khaki canvas satchel, please pass it to a member of the crew who will reunite it with its owner forthwith.'

One of the crew was descending the steps, his gaze fixed on Hector. As he drew up beside us, he crouched down to talk to Hector in a low voice.

'Excuse me, sir, I hope you don't mind me asking, but will that be your bag on your shoulder?'

Hector looked down in surprise, as if he'd just spotted that he'd grown an extra limb.

'Yes, and here's proof, if you need it.' He pointed to a battered leather luggage tag that hung from bottom of the strap. 'That's me, Hector Munro.'

For corroboration, he reached inside his jeans pocket and pulled out his wallet, from which he extracted his driving licence and held it up. The crew member raised his hand to his temple in a kind of salute.

'Thank you, sir. That's all in order, I'm sure. Sorry to have troubled you.'

'No trouble at all really,' said Hector weakly.

As he reached for my hands, I leaned into him to whisper in his ear. 'You know what that means about the man overboard?' If he hadn't been holding my hands, I've have added air quotes to that last word. 'He didn't fall, he was pushed.'

Hector's eyebrows shot up.

'What a reckless thing to do with so many witnesses.'

'Were there, though?' I looked around the cabin. 'You were the only person I've seen go on deck since the start of the cruise. Who else was up there besides you?'

Hector thought for a moment.

'Only a couple of people at the other end of the deck from me. I assumed they were birdwatchers eager to take good shots of the ospreys. I was too preoccupied with getting a decent photo of the castle in front of us to pay them much attention.'

'Well, I've got news for you, Hector. The man who fell in was dressed exactly like you. When I saw him go past the window, I thought he was you. And now we know he was also carrying the same type of bag. I'm willing to bet the culprit thought he was pushing you overboard, and that he did it to get your satchel.'

'But why? It's only cheap old army surplus kit. It's not valuable.'

I let go of his hands and folded my arms. The rain was falling so hard now that we couldn't see as much as an outline of the castle, or even the shore.

'No, silly. It's what he thought was in it that mattered. It's all starting to make sense now. Someone is after your bag, and they are prepared to go to any lengths to get it. Presumably he thought you were still carrying it around with you, as you were yesterday.'

Hector narrowed his eyes.

'But why? There's nothing in there of any value. I keep my

wallet in my jacket pocket and my phone in the pocket of my jeans. All I've got in my bag is my water bottle, a notebook and pen, a packet of mints, and, at the moment, your mum's book. Which makes it the most valuable item in there, but that's not saying much. We know it's only worth a fiver. Mr McNab told us that.'

I shrugged.

'What does Mr McNab know? He's just taking it at face value as a book. There's got to be more to it than that. Perhaps at the Highland Outdoor Heritage Museum their historians will be able to tell us what makes it so covetable.'

The engine noise subsided a little as we returned at a slower pace. Hector and I fell silent, conscious that our fellow passengers might now be able to hear us even if we whispered.

By the time we reached the harbour, the general chatter of speculation had been replaced by grudging discussions of whether to plump for refunds or new tickets. As the crew secured the boat to sturdy metal bollards on the harbourside, all the passengers' eyes were on the ambulance parked beside the ticket kiosk. The minute the gangplank clunked down into place, people began to get to their feet. As they did so, the tannoy crackled into action once more.

'Ladies and gentlemen, boys and girls, please allow our damp friend here to disembark first and make his way to the emergency services vehicle. Please be assured that this is the first incident of its kind on our cruise line, and we trust it will be our last. On disembarkation, please form an orderly queue at the ticket office where my bonny colleagues, Fiona and Kirsty will be delighted to process your refunds or supply alternative tickets.'

'I bet they won't,' I murmured to Hector. 'Be pleased, I mean. Some of our fellow passengers are sounding really disgruntled. I bet they'll give poor Fiona and Kirsty hell. Which shall we go for? Refund or repeat trip?'

Hector gazed back up the loch for a moment.

'I think we've been there, done that now, haven't we, Sophie?'

I nodded.

'We can always drive to Castle Urquhart another day if you change your mind. But what I'd like to do now is just go home and get warm and dry. This holiday is starting to feel like a Highland game of Cluedo. Everywhere we go there is a mysterious man waiting to harm you. But who is he and why is he after you?'

'Actually, I don't think there can be, sweetheart. Whoever was messing about at McNab's and the swimming pool – and it may well have been two different people – there's no way he or they could have known we'd be taking a cruise on Loch Ness today. We didn't even know ourselves until this morning.'

Reassuring words, but Hector's face was stern as he watched the ambulance drive away.

25

AROUND TOWN

'For goodness' sake, don't tell my mum about the man overboard, whatever you do.'

We slipped our coats off and hung them over the backs of two kitchen chairs to dry. Hector shook his curls out like a dog after a swim. The drizzle had made his hair go quite fluffy, and I reached up to run my fingers through it to redefine the waves.

Hector put his arms round me and kissed my forehead.

'Don't worry, sweetheart. I wasn't planning to. It would just reinforce her fears about going up on deck.' He pulled me against him for a hug. 'It must be tough being the parents of an only child. At least my mum and dad have got a spare.'

I appreciated his trying to normalise my mum's anxiety, especially as I knew that when he was a boy, he very nearly had ended up as an only child. His twin brother Horace had contracted childhood leukaemia and only pulled through after a long course of treatment. The impact on both had left a lasting mark on their personalities. Ironically, Horace, having nearly lost his life, was the risk-taker, as if his recovery had somehow made him indestructible. Hector was the more cautious, sensible one.

Now that we were back home safe, I could feel a touch of delayed shock kicking in, and I started to tremble. I tried to cover up my own anxiety by making light of the situation.

'Does that mean I have a spare too? If this madman catches up with you, can I transfer my affections to Horace as a substitute?'

'Only if a crocodile doesn't get him first.'

'Given his edgy existence in Oz, it would be ironic if you went first, wouldn't it?'

Hector grimaced. 'I'm not sure I like the way this conversation is going, sweetheart.'

'Sorry, Hector,' I said, as I filled the kettle. 'I think the events of the last few days are making me a bit morbid.'

'So what do we tell your parents about today? We should agree our official story before they get home tonight. They're bound to ask how we got on.'

'Okay, so our official story is that we had a nice round trip on the boat but decided not to go into the castle because it was raining so hard. We might drive to Castle Urquhart later in the week if we can fit it in. That would also give us time to see the exhibition at the Loch Ness Centre on the same day. It's more or less opposite, but the cruise timetable doesn't allow you to fit it in before your return trip, so it's an advantage in a way.

'Mum and Dad won't be home until about six o'clock anyway. We should be feeling much calmer by then and better able to – well, to lie.'

Hector pulled out a chair from the kitchen table and sat down to remove his suede boots, now much darkened by the rain.

'It strikes me you're keeping a lot from your parents.'

I shrugged. 'I worked out long ago that it's best to tell my mum things on a need-to-know basis.'

'Then they can't know much, especially as they've never been to visit you in Wendlebury since you inherited May's cottage. I thought they were very close to her and might like to return. Or is it that they can't bear to visit without her being there?'

I chose two pretty, floral-patterned, bone-china cups and saucers from the shelf, a remnant from the hotel's old tea-service.

'They were close, especially my dad, as she was his blood relation. My mum is only her niece by marriage.' I paused to spoon loose tea into the matching teapot. 'The real problem is that my mum no longer travels unless she absolutely needs to.'

Hector's jaw dropped. 'What, not even for holidays?'

The kettle reached boiling point and switched itself off.

'No, not for a long time. Not since Suzy, really. She's got as far as the airport or the train station once or twice, then found some last-minute excuse to turn back. Auntie May's funeral may be the only time she's left Scotland since Suzy's accident.'

I lifted the teapot lid to hasten the brewing process with a quick stir.

'Ironic when you consider Auntie May effectively travelled for a living, given that she was a travel writer. Before Suzy died, we travelled so much as a family, moving around for Mum and Dad's jobs, and taking holidays. Plus Dad has his Munro-bagging, and Mum and I used to go with him to drop him off at his starting point, then we'd go off to do something touristy like visiting museums or taking boat trips while he was hillwalking, then we'd pick him up again at the end of the day. I've seen far more of Scotland than most Scots. I was also pretty well trav-elled between university and moving to May's cottage. Mum's refusal to travel might even have been a factor in my decision to work abroad – I wanted to make up for lost time.'

Hector got up to fetch the milk from the fridge while I poured tea into the cups and took them to the table.

'But she seemed keen enough to go to the Highland Outdoor Heritage Museum. Wouldn't you count that as travel?'

'It's less than an hour's drive, so hardly adventurous. It may not happen, though, so don't get your hopes up. I keep hoping that Mum will regain her confidence, and Dad and I have always done our best to support and encourage her, but nothing's worked, and she won't even consider seeking counselling.'

Hector added milk to our tea before raising his cup to his lips.

'That's tough on your dad.'

'Far tougher on Dad than on me. I've been able to go off on my own travels, but Dad doesn't want to go away on holiday without Mum. And now of course she's stopped him hillwalking too. At first I didn't travel either, but Auntie May encouraged me to, and after hearing so much about her adventures when I used to visit her in the summer holidays as a child, I didn't take much persuading.'

Hector set his cup down carefully on the saucer, probably conscious this crockery would break far more easily than the chunky kind we used in the tearoom at Hector's House.

'You lived and worked in some interesting places abroad too, didn't you? Most recently Frankfurt?'

'I know, and it's such a shame Mum and Dad never visited me in any of them. Dad always misses out because he stays to take care of Mum, like the type who doesn't want to take a holiday because they don't want to put their dog into kennels.'

Hector spluttered mid-sip and set his cup back down on the saucer.

'Bit harsh, Sophie, comparing your mum to a dog.'

I grimaced. 'Sorry. Anyway, now you can see why I don't want to tell them anything that might alarm them. I don't want to set back Mum any further. I'm hopeful that she might travel again one day. She used to love travelling when I was little. We had some lovely family holidays abroad and on some of the Scottish islands. But I'm not holding my breath.'

I drained my cup, set it down on its saucer and went to check the weather out of the kitchen window.

'Oh, look, a rainbow! Quick, or you'll miss it.' I waved to him to join me. 'Look, the clouds are moving away rapidly now. We'll have clear blue sky in a minute.'

Hector scraped his chair back and got to his feet.

'Well, that was a quick change. Judging by how grim the weather was when we got back, I'd assumed we'd be spending the rest of the day indoors.'

He stood behind me and clasped his arms around my waist, resting his chin on my shoulder. I leaned back against him, comfortable.

'Auntie May always said there are four seasons in Scotland, and you get them all on the same day. Let's take advantage of the sunshine while it lasts and go for a bike ride beside the Caledonian Canal. We can cross the river at Ness Islands, follow it to Whin Park and grab an ice cream, then cycle along the towpath to where the canal meets the Beauly Firth.'

Hector went to collect our coats from the chairs.

'We won't need those now,' I said. 'We just need to grab the cycle helmets from the shed, and the bikes, of course. We'll probably have to dust them off a bit, as Mum and Dad never use them these days. But it'll be fun.'

Hector followed me out of the back door to the shed at the bottom of the garden.

'I suppose your mum wouldn't be keen on the idea of this trip, either? It sounds as if we'll be beside water all the way.'

I twiddled the dial on the coded padlock of the shed door.

'She won't know until we get back anyway. Actually, it'll be good for her. Although she'd have worried like mad beforehand if she knew that was our plan, she'll realise when we've come back safe and sound that she needn't have worried at all. Positive reinforcement.'

I grabbed an old towel that hung from a nail on the back of the shed door and dusted down the saddles, handlebars and helmets. As I did so, I realised I'd never been on a cycle ride with Hector before either. I hoped he wasn't about to tell me he didn't know how to ride a bike.

26

ON THE TOWPATH

'Aargh!' Hector shrieked as we cycled across the rickety Infirmary Bridge, but this time he was only messing about rather than being genuinely unnerved. Gleefully, I joined in. Soon we were whizzing along the far bank of the Ness. As we passed Ness Islands on our left, I drew my bike alongside his and shouted across the gap between us.

'The islands don't look anywhere near as eerie in daylight, do they?'

'No, and they're just as pretty in daylight, especially with this touch of autumn colour just starting to appear.'

I smiled, glad that he was warming to one of my favourite parts of the city.

'That's the National Archives Office coming up on our right,' I called, pointing to a neat, modern building set back slightly from the road. 'We could look up your man from the Gaelic book inscription there, if you like, and pinpoint his where-abouts. Although there'll likely be dozens with the same name on Lewis. Names used to get passed down the generations like heirlooms over there. Sometimes all the brothers in a family would take their father's or grandfather's name, like Donald, with a middle name or nickname to differentiate them, according to their personality or their trade – Donald Fish or Donald Ferry, for instance. It must have got awfully confusing in the classroom when the children were little. It still happens on the mainland to a certain extent. My mum and dad are friends with an elderly man in Cromarty named Eric, who's known in his family as Big Eric, his son as Young Eric and his grandson as Wee Eric, although he's nearly as old as me now.'

We were pedalling at exactly the same rate, the cycling equivalent of synchronised swimmers.

'I'm glad my parents didn't take that approach,' Hector called back to me. 'It was bad enough being identical twins with the same initials.'

'But think of the saving on school name labels,' I joked. 'Still, in the tough crofting communities of the Highlands and Islands, traditions like that were important, far more so than in somewhere soft like the Cotswolds.'

'Crofting, that's like smallholding, isn't it?'

As we reached the gates of the park, we dismounted and parked our bikes by the entrance.

'It's a bit more complicated than that. Sometimes crofts are owned outright, but there are very strict laws controlling how the land is passed on. I'm not familiar with the details, but it's one of the things Mum lectures on. I suppose it's a throwback to the Highland Clearances, when the new English landlords chucked so many peasants off their land. That would make you ultra-cautious after that about hanging on to your property and keeping out interlopers, don't you think?'

The school day had not yet ended, and the ice-cream seller seemed very pleased to see us. He can't have done much trade during the morning's downpour.

Hector bought us each a 99, and we strolled towards the playpark, where we sat on a bench, from which all traces of the morning's rain had been banished by the sun, now shining away in clear blue sky.

'Hear that tooting?' I paused, halfway through eating the chocolate flake. 'That shows the miniature railway is still running. We can go for a ride after we've finished this if you like. Or else take a boat out.' I pointed across to the lake, where the hire attendant was sprawling in a deckchair, soaking up the sun. He'd probably also been short of customers that morning, but was clearly taking advantage of the perks of his job before the season ended. 'Although we've probably had enough of boats for one day.'

'Let's take the train,' agreed Hector.

Once I'd licked the last of the ice cream out of my cone, I crumbled it up to scatter on the grass, to the delight of a few mallards who waddled over as fast they could, quacking in gratitude.

Spending an hour in the playpark in the afternoon sunshine was just what we needed to restore our spirits after our earlier drama. When we climbed astride one of the train's tiny carriages, and I leaned against Hector's warm back, clasping my arms around his waist, I felt safe. All my worries of the last couple of days fell away. Of course, it was easy to trip on a spiral staircase, and Mr McNab had hinted that it was his cleaner's fault for polishing them. No wonder Hector struggled in the whirlpool when he couldn't swim. Most likely no one ducked him on purpose. The blow he felt was probably just someone accidentally colliding with him after emerging from the tunnel feeding into that pool. Perhaps his wristband was much looser than mine and had slipped off under the force of the various water jets along the slide. It was my own silly fault for not realising he couldn't swim, or I'd never have taken him down the Spiral. Okay, maybe a little bit his fault too for not telling me, but no real harm had been done. Of course, the man on the deck of the motor cruiser had just fallen by accident. The deck was slippery in the rain, and that was exactly why the crew had encouraged us to stay below. He was probably just trying to sneak an illicit cigarette and lost his footing while concentrating on his subterfuge. Served him right!

My goodness, I was worrying about nothing. Was I turning into my mum?

I leaned in a little closer to Hector, remembering the pleasant trips I'd taken on this little train with Mum and Dad for as long as we'd lived in Inverness. When I was long past the stage of sitting on Dad's lap or holding Mum's hand to cross the road, we'd stroll down here sometimes at the weekend, bringing a picnic. The excuse for physical closeness, on the pretext of safety, was precious, even in my teens.

'Look out for the elephant!' I shouted to Hector over his shoulder, pointing at the big grey model lurking in the undergrowth.

'Beware of the hippo!' he called back, as we rounded a bend and encountered another huge statue.

By the time the little train drew to a halt in the station after its circular journey, we were laughing like children. We staggered slightly as we dismounted after sitting astride the carriage for so long.

Once we were back on our bikes, I led the way to the towpath of the Caledonian Canal, and soon we were cycling gently along in the sunshine, still water on one side and hedgerows laden with ripe blackberries on the other. We waved to the little sailboats gliding past under engine power, heading for the sea, some of them probably about to raise their sails for the first time in days after traversing the length of Thomas Telford's magnificent canal that slices Scotland so neatly in half.

With a little extra effort, we cycled up a small incline to the road, crossed it, and freewheeled down to rejoin the towpath on the other side. A minute later, I heard a shout of alarm behind me, and I braked to a halt before looking back over my shoulder to find its cause.

Sprawled across the towpath was Hector, one leg trapped beneath his bike, which lay parallel to the path, its front wheel and his head and shoulders hanging out over the water.

At once I turned my bike around and pedalled back to his rescue. As I did so, a spindly old lady on a vintage-style bicycle teetered towards me, apparently unaware of Hector's plight. If he had fallen after she had passed him, and she was deaf, she might be oblivious of his accident, or had she caused it, and cycled blithely on? Was it an accident or – I gulped at the thought – sabotage?

All along I'd been picturing a strong man as Hector's assailant, which is why I wouldn't have taken any notice of an old lady at McNab's, at the swimming pool or on the boat. Yes, there had been an old lady on the scene at each of the previous incidents.

I dismounted and set my bike on its kickstand, before lifting Hector's bike off his leg and hoicking it aside. I was relieved we'd been wearing cycling helmets, although as his head didn't seem to have hit the ground when he fell, protective headgear may not have made any material difference.

Hector scrambled to his feet and stretched his arms and legs to check for damage, before brushing the mud and damp gravel off his jeans.

'Whatever happened then?' I glanced back at the elderly lady, now a speck in the distance. 'Did that old woman cut you up? Don't tell me she deliberately tried to shove you in the water!'

I gazed into the canal's depths, trying not to picture how much worse the accident might have been.

Hector held up a grazed hand, dark with blood and embedded dust and gravel.

'I thought we'd left all your conspiracy theories behind us,' he protested. 'Anyway, I'm sure it was an innocent accident. I'd slowed down a bit to watch some ducks hopping from the bank into the canal, and her front wheel just touched my back one. That was enough to make my bike change course and veer towards the water. I guess it was my fault for slowing down without giving a hand signal to warn anyone behind me. She was probably concentrating too hard on staying upright herself to notice what had happened to me.'

'Which was?'

Hector bent to inspect his bike's back wheel, gripping the brake callipers between thumb and forefinger and squeezing them a few times.

'When I realised I was headed straight for the water, my immediate instinct was to brake hard, but the brakes didn't respond. So, I twisted the handlebars quick to redirect the bike back to the right to stay on the towpath. But I must have over-compensated, because I lost my balance and fell off.'

I knelt on the path beside his bike and followed the brake cable with my forefinger from the handlebars to the callipers.

'No wonder the brakes didn't work. Look, the cable's snapped.'

'Surely not.' He peered at where I was pointing. 'I hope you're not going to tell me you think that little old lady sneaked a knife out while she was passing and severed the cable. Or that she had knives sticking out of her wheels, like some super-competitive Ancient Roman gladiator, or a character in *Wacky Races*.'

I frowned. 'Of course not. But don't you think it seems odd that they were working fine before she came on the scene?'

Hector took one of the ends of the cable between thumb and forefinger and turned its cut surface towards him to examine it more closely. 'I suppose it's a question of the last straw. If the cable was already a bit decayed from lack of use, the sudden force that I applied when I braked hard might have been enough to sever it. You said your parents hadn't used the bikes for years. So, it may have been the old lady's fault indirectly, for cutting me up, but that doesn't make her a crazed assassin.'

I was trying hard to believe him.

'Anyway, whatever the cause, we can't carry on cycling now. Even if I took it very slowly, it would be foolhardy to ride without a working brake. Are there any shops near here where we can buy a replacement cable?'

I thought for a moment.

'If we head back to where we crossed the road and turn left, I'm pretty sure there's a bike shop along there somewhere on the way into town. It's a bit of a trek, but I don't see what else we can do. At least it's still early enough for us to pick up a new cable and fit it before Mum and Dad get home. We can still tell them we had a lovely bike ride without mentioning this little incident.'

Hector winced as he put his hands on his handlebars to turn his bike back towards the way we had come. The grazes on his palms must have been very sore. He adjusted his grip to steer the bike using only his fingertips, and we began to trudge back towards the road.

'Then I'll take you to my favourite café and you can wash

your hands and clean up in their bathroom,' I suggested, encouragingly.

As we turned at the top of the slope, I glanced back to see whether there was any sign of the old lady. Cyclists often double back once they reach the Beauly Firth, but she was nowhere to be seen.

27

I SHOULD COCOA

'That brake cable hasna snapped, it's been cut,' said the balding
mechanic in dark-blue overalls. He ran a hand over his gleaming
pate, crowned with a black headtorch on an elastic band,
smearing it with oily dust. 'Or at least cut part-way across.'

'The bike's been lying unused in my parents' shed for years,'
I admitted. 'Mightn't it just have perished?'

He detached the cable and held up the severed ends for us to
see. 'Och, no, dear. Look, the casing's been cut with a knife or
scissors. It's a neat edge, not a ragged result of wear and tear or
of natural decomposition.' He sucked his teeth for a moment.
'Perishing would leave cracks and splits, not a neat edge.' He
switched on his headtorch and aimed it at the cable. 'Looks to
me as if someone's tried to sever the cable but with insufficient
force, or with an inadequate instrument. Kitchen scissors or nail
clippers, perhaps, instead of wire cutters. They've hacked
through the casing before giving it up as a bad job. Might even
have broken their scissors. That'll teach 'em. As I'm sure you
realise, brake cables are very strong, but if you trash their casing

and leave them exposed to cold damp air and don't oil 'em, they'll rust, and it's only a matter of time before they'll snap.'

He tapped a patch of rust accusingly, sending orange specks cascading onto the grimy concrete floor.

'Still, you're in luck, sir. We've plenty of brake cables in stock.'

He pulled out a red plastic storage box from beneath the trade counter, lifted the lid, and rummaged among an assortment of little square plastic packages to find the right size. He pulled one out with a flourish.

'Here you go, sir. That'll be £7.49, please.'

He dropped it onto the counter. As Hector slipped his hand into his jeans pocket to pull out his wallet, he flinched at the pressure on his grazed palm. The mechanic nodded at his hand as he withdrew it.

'You want to get that cleaned up sooner rather than later. You're welcome to use the lavatory at the back of the shop. Run your hands under the tap for a bit to wash out any foreign bodies, but best not to use the hand towel. It's a bit grubby and will do you more harm than good. But at least you can rinse off any surface dirt, and the cold water will soothe the swelling.'

I encouraged Hector with a gentle nudge.

'Go on, Hector. I'll settle up while you do what the man says.'

I dug in my bag for my purse and tapped my debit card on the countertop card reader.

'Nasty fall, was it, dear?' asked the mechanic, handing me the receipt.

As I tried to smile in gratitude at his concern, my eyes were filling with tears.

'Here, I tell you what, dear, it's all quiet here this afternoon. You take that boy of yours and get him a nice cup of tea, and I'll fit the cable for him. You look like you could do with a brew. I'll have the bike ready for you by five. You can leave your bike here too, if you like. It'll be safe enough.'

This time I managed to smile.

'Thanks, that's really kind of you. And I know exactly where I'm going to take him.'

* * *

'I Should Cocoa?' Hector laughed at the name of my favourite café as I pushed open the big old-fashioned wooden door, part of the original Victorian shop fittings. 'Sounds like the choco-holic's equivalent of an opium den.'

I gave a guilty grin.

'You're not far wrong there, Hector. When I was in my last couple of years at senior school, I had a Saturday job here, and they might just as well have paid me in kind, I spent so much of my wages on chocolate. Their drinks and cakes are completely addictive.'

I led us to a booth at the back of the shop, my favourite spot to take my break when I worked there. We sat facing each other on either side of the table and picked up the menu cards, although I already knew what I was going to have – cocoa, topped with whipped cream and hundreds and thousands, and garnished with spun sugar. Hector picked a more pedestrian pot of English breakfast tea, but I didn't criticise, thinking it would be good for shock. But when I went to the counter to order our drinks, I chose two very indulgent chocolate brownies, one with honeycomb and the other with rum and ginger.

None of the staff behind the counter were familiar faces, and I felt a pang of disappointment that I was no longer part of the team here. Then I saw Hector smiling at me warmly as I returned carrying the cakes and remembered I belonged to a different team now. I put both cakes down on his side of the table and slid onto the banquette beside him.

'Is it okay to touch you now?' I enquired, laying my left hand gently on his thigh. 'I'm not sure where your latest bruises are. You're amassing quite a collection. I don't want to hurt you further.'

Hector put his arm around me and pulled me closer. 'It's a risk I'm prepared to take,' he replied, although he kept his fingers curled protectively over his sore palm, rather than laying it flat on my shoulder as he normally would.

We were silent for a moment, perhaps still regaining our equilibrium after the upset of the bike ride.

'So, do you still think the old woman was innocent?' I asked as a young waitress in school shirt and trousers beneath her chocolate-brown apron set our drinks in front of us.

I poured Hector's cup of tea to save him putting any unnecessary stress on his sore hands. He turned his brownie around on his tea plate with his cake fork, as if considering which side to tackle first.

'I'm sure the old lady had no murderous intentions on me, if that's what you mean,' he said, cutting off a corner of the brownie with a sharp edge of the fork before spearing it with its tiny prongs. 'If she really wanted me to end up in the canal, she could easily have made a much better job of it. No, it's my fault, sweetheart. I don't know why I didn't signal to show my intention of slowing down. I'd never make a manoeuvre in my Land Rover without signalling. I guess I'm just out of practice at cycling. Shame really, as I was enjoying it until then. Still, like falling off a horse, we must get back in the saddle as soon as we collect the bikes from the repair shop. I'm sure we'll have a nice ride home. But I'd still like to know who cut the cable, and why.' He hesitated. 'I don't like to say this, Sophie, but is there anyone who has a grudge against your dad? After all, I was riding your dad's bike. Your mum's was fine.'

I lifted the golden swirl of spun sugar off the top of my cocoa and stirred the whipped cream with a teaspoon, creating a kaleidoscope of colour as the hundreds and thousands sprinkled on the top began to dissolve.

'What, you mean like a disgruntled student? I suppose that's a possibility. Perhaps someone getting a lower grade than he thought he merited, although that would seem a drastic way to eke his revenge. Criminal, in fact. If Dad had been cycling through Inverness in the middle of the rush hour when the cable snapped, he could have ended up under a bus.' I picked up the spun sugar disc to take a bite, but then laid it on my cake plate, feeling a little queasy. 'It certainly couldn't have happened while the bike was locked in the shed at home, but it's a very long time since Mum or Dad cycled to work. If it was a resentful student, he'd have graduated or dropped out long ago, so there'll be no chance of catching him now.'

'Or her,' said Hector. He put another piece of brownie in his mouth. 'My goodness, that's delicious!' He was so eager to express his appreciation that he spoke through a mouthful of crumbs. 'In any case,' he continued, once his mouth was empty, 'I don't think there's any connection between this and my previous two accidents this week. Goodness, I thought this was meant to be a holiday, not an assault course.' Seeing my crestfallen face, he patted my knee in reassurance. 'Don't worry, I'm enjoying it really. I'm just glad we didn't opt for a fortnight. I'm not sure I'd live to tell the tale. Besides, now I've had three accidents, that should be it. You know what they say about trouble coming in threes.'

I really wanted to believe him, although I was no more superstitious than he was. Falling silent, we applied ourselves to the rest of our cakes.

28

UNFORESEEN CIRCUMSTANCES

* * *

'"Closed early due to unforeseen circumstances",' I read from the handwritten sign on the bicycle shop door. '"Open again at 9 a.m. tomorrow".'

Hector tutted.

'We could have come back earlier if we'd known instead of pottering about the City Museum to kill time after we'd had our tea and cake.'

'We should have left a mobile number.' I swung my helmet by its strap. 'Although to be fair, there didn't seem to be the need. Oh well, I guess we'll just have to come back in the morning. As it's nearly five o'clock now and we'll have to walk back; we'll be lucky to get home before Mum and Dad. If we turn up carrying our helmets, they'll know we've been cycling, and we'll have to tell them about the accident. Bother. We should have left them with the bikes.'

'If we go in the back way, can't we just leave them in the shed? They'll have come in the front door, as they drove to work, so they probably won't see us.'

We turned away from the shop and started to walk in the direction of home.

'You know, Sophie, I think you're being overcautious trying to protect your parents so much, or rather, your mum,' continued Hector. 'Don't you think you're in danger of being an enabler?'

That took me aback.

'Well, that's harsh, but probably true. You're right, Hector. We must tell them. I'm being overprotective. It'll be a lesson to them to look after their bikes better.'

* * *

We waited until we were all sitting around the dining table tucking into haggis, neeps and tatties before raising the issue with Mum and Dad.

'Here's a real Scottish supper for you, son,' Dad enthused, pouring Mum's rich gravy over fluffy orange and white mounds of mashed vegetables. 'We'll make a true Munro out of you yet.'

I was unsure whether to be pleased that dad had taken to calling Hector 'son' or alarmed that he seemed bent on turning him into someone he was not. What was wrong with my lovely English Hector?

Once we'd all finished passing round the gravy jug and Dad had filled wine glasses for himself, Hector, and me – Mum's was already full of water – he raised a traditional Scottish toast: 'Lang may yer lum reek!'

Hector smiled companionably at my dad and raised his glass in return.

'Och aye the noo!' he replied in a comedy high-pitched Scottish accent, making us all laugh.

'So how was your boat trip today, you two?' asked Mum, after we'd taken a first sip from our glasses. There was a slight tremor in her voice.

'Oh, fine,' I said quickly. 'But we decided not to get off at Castle Urquhart as the weather was so gloomy.'

'Altogether dreich.' Hector looked pleased with himself for using a truly Scottish description.

There was palpable relief in Mum's voice. 'Yes, best save the castle for a fine day, when you can enjoy the view in all its glory, rather than shrouded in drizzle and mist.'

'That's what we thought,' I added hastily, hoping that the man overboard would not be reported in Dad's newspaper next morning. 'So, we came back and got your old bikes out instead.'

Mum dropped her fork with a clatter onto the parquet floor. Flustered, she bent to pick it up and rushed out to the kitchen to get another.

'You know, I miss our family bike rides,' said Dad, taking advantage of Mum's absence to drain his glass and refill it. 'When Sophie was little, the three of us often used to go cycling together. It's conveniently flat around here, perhaps surprisingly so, considering we're in the capital of the Highlands, and there are some delightful outings within easy reach. The canal towpath in both directions, for example.'

'That's where we went today,' said Hector, 'after an enjoyable jaunt to Whin Park.'

Dad took a long draught from his glass and refilled it. I looked away, embarrassed at how much he was drinking.

'Remember our train rides around Whin Park and the boats on the boating lake?' Dad sat down his glass at last. 'Ah, happy days!'

'We went on the miniature railway too,' I told him.

Dad gazed at me fondly for a moment.

'Ah, well, you're never too old for a miniature railway. It's just who you go with that changes, isn't it, love? Oh well, maybe I'll get to go again when grandchildren come along.'

I was relieved that Mum chose that moment to return, lest Dad completely embarrass me by asking Hector whether his intentions were honourable.

'So did you have a nice bike ride, love?' asked Dad. 'We used to cycle that route for picnics. Do you remember?'

'It was lovely, thanks. And yes, Mum, before you ask, we wore your helmets.'

Mum drained her glass of water, and to my surprise, refilled it from the wine bottle. Was this just a tactic to stop dad from drinking so much? Would she even drink it? She did, taking a large gulp straight away.

'We haven't used those old bikes for years,' Dad continued. 'It would be suicidal to cycle to work these days with so much traffic on our route to campus. I would only ever use mine these days when hillwalking.'

'You cycle up mountains on that bike?' Hector was wide-eyed. 'But it's hardly a mountain bike.'

Dad chuckled. 'Bless you, no, only to access the starting point of a Munro trail. Some of the Munros are many miles from the road and a long trudge across footpaths. Even if you're tackling them during the long daylight hours in summer, it helps to do that first stretch on a bike. Gives you more daylight hours on the hill.'

Mum stared at her plate.

'So did you enjoy your bike ride too, Hector?' Her voice was trembling.

Hector and I exchanged glances, and I gave him a slight nod of complicity.

'It was terrific, thanks, apart from one tiny hiccup, but we've resolved that now,' he said.

When he held up his hand in a kind of stop gesture to indicate closure, Mum reached across the table, grasped his fingers and turned his palm over to inspect it.

'You've hurt yourself, Hector. How did that happen?'

He withdrew his palm to inspect it himself.

'Oh, don't worry, it's just a graze. I'm afraid I took a tumble on the towpath. Nothing serious.'

I was anxious to show Hector in a chivalric light, rather than making him seem incompetent.

'He was making way for a doddery old lady on an ancient old-fashioned bike. It's not his fault his brake cable snapped.'

Mum choked slightly on her mouthful of mashed potato, which seemed an odd thing to choke on.

'But don't worry,' I said quickly, hoping to put her at her ease. 'We've taken it to that little bicycle repair shop in town, and the kind man in there said he'd replace it for us for only the cost of the part. I think he was a bit bored and welcomed something to do. We left both bikes there and walked into town. We'll go back and collect them in the morning. Then we had afternoon tea at I Should Coco. Isn't that nice?'

Dad chuckled again.

'I'm surprised that café's still in business since you left. Their profits must have taken quite a dive when you moved away.'

I gave a sheepish smile.

'It was lovely to be back. Although I didn't see anyone I knew there, just waitresses with school uniforms under their pinnies, just like I used to be, except when I did the weekend shift.'

I turned to Hector.

'Maybe we should ask Mrs Wetherley to make more fancy brownies like theirs, and I could make more exotic drinks.'

Hector smiled proudly at my dad.

'Sophie's full of good ideas for my bookshop and tearoom. I can't tell you how glad I am to have her on my staff.'

'On your staff?' I laughed drily. 'I am your staff. There's not exactly a cast of thousands at Hector's House, is there?'

'Sorry, sweetheart, that came out wrong. I just want to let your mum and dad know what a difference you've made to my business as well as to me personally.'

Dad raised his glass to me and winked.

'Sounds like a good time to ask him for a pay rise, love.'

I turned to Mum for her opinion, hoping to see her looking proud of me, but this conversation seemed to be passing her by.

'The brake cable,' she murmured. 'Are you sure it was the brake cable that was the trouble?'

'Absolutely sure, Mum. It was completely severed. The bicycle mechanic showed us the cut bit. He said it was a wonder it hadn't been snapped sooner.'

Dad laid his knife and fork down on his empty plate.

'Well, you've done me a service, Hector. Just imagine what would have happened if I'd got halfway along a deserted mountain path only to fall off and knock myself out on a rock. Sometimes I can go a whole day on the hill without seeing another soul.'

'And you wonder why I don't want you to go Munro-ing,' said Mum, getting up as if to remove the empty plates but first taking the wine bottle, which was not yet empty, out to the kitchen and thus out of Dad's reach.

I followed her, a serving dish in each hand, and set them on the draining board. Mum slumped down on a kitchen chair and buried her face in her hands. Her shoulders began to shake.

'Why didn't you tell me you were planning on taking those old bikes out? I could have warned you.'

I pulled out the chair next to hers and sat down before putting my arms around her shoulders. For the first time, I felt like I was parenting my parents.

'What is it, Mum? What's bothering you? Would it help to tell me?'

She leaned her head on my shoulder, and I pulled her into a closer embrace.

'Sophie, can you forgive me? Please don't tell Dad.' She raised her head just enough to glance up at the door and reassure herself that he wasn't in earshot. 'It was me. It was me that cut the brake cable. I sabotaged Dad's bike to stop him going up any more hills.'

'You did what?'

I could hardly believe what I was hearing.

'I thought he'd notice the brakes weren't working as he wheeled it out of the shed and just give up on his trip as a bad job.'

'But, Mum, you hadn't cut them right through. You hadn't severed the metal cable, only the plastic casing. The brakes were working fine when we left, but it was only a matter of time till the cable gave way. It could have snapped at any time, including when Dad was miles from anywhere, with no phone signal and little chance of passers-by to come to his aid.'

Mum went silent for a moment, and when she spoke again, her voice was ragged.

'Sophie, please know that I only did it because I love him so much. You do realise that, don't you? Those precious hills of his are so dangerous. I couldn't bear to lose him too.'

She gave a strangled cry, unable to speak any further, and I laid her head on my shoulder and put my arms about her, as she began to sob.

'I know that, Mum,' I said gently. 'But you really must tell Dad too.'

And perhaps get counselling at last, I thought to myself, before you get the chance to do Dad or anyone else serious harm with your misguided actions. But first, she needed to come clean with Dad.

'How about we all go to the pictures tonight?' Dad said as I returned to fetch the empty plates. 'I was just saying to Hector what a great facility we've got at the theatre just across the river.'

'What's on?' I asked, stacking the plates and piling the knives and forks on top. I wasn't sure whether Mum would be up for an outing given the state she was in when I left the kitchen. On the other hand, maybe sitting in the dark would give her a welcome opportunity to hide her face while it recovered from the after-effects of crying.

Dad pulled his phone out of his jacket pocket and punched in a search string.

'*Touching the Void*. Hmm, I don't think that would get your mother's vote. Or they're doing a classic black and white season. Tonight, it's Laurel and Hardy in *The Music Box*.'

'That sounds good to me.' I turned to Hector. 'What do you think?'

Hector was looking at me questioningly, clearly aware that something was up in the kitchen but not wanting to ask outright.

Standing behind Dad's back, I mouthed, 'I'll tell you later.'

'I'm up for that, sweetheart.'

'Can you ask Mum if she wants to go, love?' Dad sat back in his chair, replete from dinner.

'Actually, Dad, I think Mum would rather like to stay in with you tonight. There's something she needs to talk to you about.'

Dad looked faintly surprised, but didn't object.

'Okay, love, well, you and Hector have fun at the pictures. See you in a bit.'

* * *

I waited until we'd crossed the rickety bridge and were strolling up the riverbank in the dusk before telling Hector about my conversation with Mum in the kitchen.

'It was Mum,' I said flatly. 'Mum did it.'

Hector stopped in his tracks.

'Did what? Pushed me down the stairs? Ducked me in the pool?' He began to walk again, staring into the distance. 'Don't tell me that little old lady was her in disguise. If so, she had me fooled.'

So, he wasn't as dismissive as he pretended to be of my theory about a serial attacker.

'And surely it wasn't her in the pool when she hasn't been able to bring herself to swim for years. Besides, we'd have recognised her in a swimsuit. It's hardly a disguise.'

I couldn't help but laugh, despite the sombre topic.

'No, silly. Why would my mum have a vendetta against you? Besides, if she wanted to bump you off, she'd have an easy opportunity at every meal. No, I mean she cut the brake cable on Dad's bike.'

'But how did she know I was going to ride it?'

I pulled at his hand to make him move on. I didn't want to miss the start of the film.

'She didn't do it to harm you. She cut it to stop Dad using it, ages ago, apparently, in an attempt to put him off going up his Munros. He'd been talking about doing one of the more challenging ones, with a long bike ride in, and she thought if his bike was out of action, he'd have to cancel the trip. She thought she'd cut the cable right through, and that he'd realise it was unusable as soon as he took it out of the shed. She didn't realise it was still rideable. She's not very mechanically minded. As it happened, the weather turned bad and he had a change of plan, and he still doesn't know what she's done. Since then, she's upped her campaign to stop him going walking altogether. I didn't realise it, but he hasn't done any Munros for years. I had no idea it had been so long.'

Hector let go of my hand to put his arm round my shoulder, and I slipped my arm around his waist.

'I have to say, her action was pretty extreme. Like your dad said, it could have been terribly dangerous if he'd gone off on the bike and the cable had finally given out when he was miles from anywhere.'

I hugged him a little closer to me.

'She's not usually murderous by nature, I promise you.'

'To the extent that she's willing to risk a potentially fatal accident for your dad? Someone needs to point out to her that two negatives don't always make a positive.'

'Don't worry, I think it's going to be okay. It may take a while to get things back on an even keel, but she promised that while we were out tonight, she was going to talk to him about it. I'm feeling good about this. I think they're going to be okay.'

We continued in silence as we turned into the gardens surrounding the theatre complex and headed for the box office. This business with Mum had certainly taken my mind off the three attacks on Hector so far, but as we took our seats in the cinema studio and the lights went down, I reminded myself not to lower my guard.

* * *

'Well, that was fun,' beamed Hector as we emerged, blinking, into the foyer. 'I'd forgotten how good Laurel and Hardy were. My face aches from laughing so much.'

'Amazing to think how fresh their humour is when it's nearly a hundred years since that film was made, especially when you think how much the world and society has changed since then.'

We strolled hand in hand out into the garden and followed the path back to the riverbank.

'Amazing, also, to think that I've never been to the cinema with you before,' I said.

We paused at the riverside beside a lamppost, our arms around each other as we gazed back at the twinkling city lights reflected in the dark surface of the ever-flowing Ness.

'We've managed so many firsts this holiday that it makes me wonder what we've been doing with our time in Wendlebury,' observed Hector. 'Apart from all the shenanigans with poor Alasdair and my unfortunate string of accidents, it's all been rather fun, don't you think?'

I had to agree. We didn't need to be in Wendlebury Barrow or at Hector's House to feel like soulmates. We just had to be together. I gazed up at him.

'I've never slept with you for so many nights in succession before as I will have done by the time we go back down south.'

Back in the village, we usually stayed at each other's places only once every two or three nights. I reached up to clasp my hands behind his neck. 'And I must admit, I quite like it.'

'Damn me with faint praise, why don't you?' said Hector, but it wasn't just the streetlamp lighting up his face.

30

THE PICK-UP

Next day's priority was to collect the bicycles from the repair shop. The nice mechanic had been kind enough to check over Mum's bike too by way of apology for having closed early without warning.

'They're both as safe now as any bicycle can be,' he reassured us as we wheeled them out of the shop.

With relief and gratitude, we cycled back to the canal to pick up our journey where we had left off. The brisk walk from home into town, followed by the bike ride to the Beauly Firth, gave us both an appetite, so on the way back, we detoured for lunch to a little pub off the beaten track with a first-floor dining room.

There was too chilly a nip in the air to eat outside, but we were lucky enough to get a table by the window so that we could enjoy the view across the firth as we ate. The Black Isle loomed in the distance beneath a vast pale sky.

'You know, just because that bicycle business wasn't targeted at you doesn't mean there's an innocent explanation for those other events,' I said, after the bartender had set in front of us two white oval plates piled high with fish and chips so freshly cooked that they were still sizzling. 'Now that you've had time to reflect, I think you think that too.'

Hector sprinkled a generous amount of malt vinegar over the crispy golden batter.

'To be honest, I'd hoped any doubts would subside once we put enough time and distance between us and the incidents in McNab's, the swimming pool and on the boat, but I confess the fresh surge of adrenaline from that bicycle accident made me think again. As I hit the canal path and lay there, feeling dizzy, I just assumed the person responsible for the previous assaults had caught up with me at last. Which is ironic, considering that particular incident is the only one on this trip that hasn't been an act of malevolence aimed at me. But it made me realise I'd been in denial.'

I set down my fork with a chip still on it.

'You just called them assaults. So do you now think they were assaults, attacks made on purpose, rather than accidents?'

Hector set his cutlery on his plate and reached across the table to take my hands.

'Yes, I'm afraid I do. As you said yourself, I'm like a mountain goat, always sure-footed on our walks along the lanes and foot-paths back home. You often hang on to me to steady you, and I've never let you fall. I know the Cotswolds aren't exactly moun-tainous, but the paths are often uneven under foot and slippery when wet. As you put it, our hills may be like speed bumps compared to your dad's Munros, but when I was travelling with Celeste all those years ago,' I flinched at the mention of the treacherous ex-girlfriend who had made him shy away from new relationships until I came along, 'we did a fair bit of walking on mountainous territory, such as the Pyrenees, without mishap.'

Seeing my dejected expression, he added quickly, 'But I'd much rather be here in Scotland with you. Anyway, the thing is, with hindsight, I'm sure now I didn't stumble on McNab's stairs. And I'm certain I didn't just sink beneath the waters in that Spiral thing for no reason. I may not be able to swim, but the water was relatively shallow. I wasn't out of my depth. With my feet on the ground, the water only came up to my waist. Someone ducked me. I wouldn't have voluntarily put my head under the water.'

Now that Hector had admitted he thought he had been purposely attacked, to surprise, my first impulse was to contradict him. I didn't want to believe that someone was after him with malicious intent, although I knew in my heart it was true. I scrabbled for innocent explanations for the other incidents, not believing them for a moment.

'Of course, it could just have been a playful kid ducking you in the pool. Maybe someone saw your hair from behind and mistook you for his curly-headed mate. Things move so fast on that slide complex, and people land in each pool at such high speed that you could easily mix up two people with similar features. Especially with men, because they're all bare-chested. When they're waist-deep in water, you can't differentiate them by their swimming costumes as much as you can girls.'

'Unless they've got distinguishing tattoos. There were plenty of tattoos in evidence, although as you know, I don't have any myself.'

'I can easily imagine a boisterous kid launching himself upon you in jest, then, as soon as he realised it was a case of mistaken identity, scuttling off down the next slide before you could tell him off.'

Hector took a sip of his beer. 'But hang on, it's term time, and there were no school-age children on the slides.'

'It might have been a couple of immature university students larking about. They're not bound by the same kind of timetables as schoolchildren. They could easily have been spending an hour in the pool mid-afternoon, and first year students aren't much more than kids.'

Hector gazed out of the window in thought. 'Actually, the force with which I was ducked could only have come from an adult and, at risk of sounding sexist, from a strong, fit man. A student could easily have a teenage brain and a man's body.'

I toyed with a large chip, wondering whether to cut it in half.

'What about the pressure from the hand that pushed you on the stairs?'

Hector looked me in the eye, his expression solemn.

'Of equal force.'

I severed the chip. There was no fooling myself. Hector's evidence was compounding my worst fears.

'But why?' I said after I'd eaten the first half. 'Why would anyone attack you? No one knows you up here. You haven't been up here long enough for anyone to develop a grudge against you.'

Hector frowned. 'There must be a motive. One random assault by a madman would be just that, but two on the same day in different places, requiring a change of costume, does suggest an attacker with a purpose and a plan.' He took another swig from his beer. 'Someone who just happened to have their swimming gear with them. Which seems a bit unlikely.'

'But, Hector, don't you see? He didn't need to at all. Remember what I said when I discovered you'd forgotten to pack your swimming trunks? That, if need be, you could buy new ones at the swimming pool. At the reception desk, they don't just sell tickets. They flog everything you need for a swim: swimsuits, towels, shampoo, shower gel, armbands. Anyone could just turn up there completely unprepared and get kitted out on the spot.'

Hector set down his glass.

'So, the person at McNab's and the person in the pool were likely one and the same.'

'But that doesn't answer the question as to why. What would anyone gain by attacking me?'

As I sipped my diet cola, I wondered whether the fish we were eating had ever swum past the pub.

I set down my glass. 'Theft. We know from the incident on the boat that he wanted to steal your satchel. And the only remarkable thing in it was Mum's Gaelic book. Unless there was anything worth having in your notebook? Like the manuscript of your next romantic novel?'

Hector laughed. 'That's a flattering thought, sweetheart, but I don't think my golden words are worth any thief taking such risks. Besides, no one but you and my family know that I'm the alter ego of romantic novelist Hermione Minty. No, my money's on your mum's book, even though I've already established with Mr McNab that the book isn't worth much.'

'Nor is it in short supply. Your attacker could have had any one of half a dozen copies off the shelves for a fiver apiece. Why attack a stranger in the middle of a busy shop for such a low-value item? Why didn't he just shoplift a copy off the shelf? He probably would have got away with it. There were no other shop assistants on duty apart from Mr McNab at the trade counter downstairs, and if there were any security cameras rolling, Mr McNab didn't seem to be looking at their footage. There were no surveillance screens on his desk. Customers would have been more likely to notice someone shoving you down the stairs of the shop than slipping a small slim book into his pocket. Far easier than following us to the swimming pool to break into your locker.'

We pondered on this conundrum while we finished eating

our lunch. Hector was the first to lay his knife and fork on his empty plate

'They didn't break in; they used the key. It was an extraordinary stroke of luck for them that they found my locker key in the pool when I lost it.'

I reached across the table for his hands.

'But I don't think you did lose it. You definitely had it on before you went down the first slide. I know, because your locker key scratched my back slightly when you put your arm round me as we were going up all those stairs. Then I think it was stolen off you on your way down the slide.' I sat up straighter as the solution came to me. 'What would be your first physical reaction if someone ducked you underwater when you weren't expecting it? What would you do with your arms?' I answered my own question by stretching my arms up over my head. 'You'd reach up, wouldn't you? You'd reach for the surface for something to pull yourself up on.' Especially as a non-swimmer, I thought, but I didn't say that aloud so as not to embarrass him. 'With your arms above the surface and your face still underwater, and you in panic mode, he could easily slip your wristband off without you realising and dash down the slide to the next level while you were recovering.'

Hector bit his lip.

'Then he'd leave the pool and raid my locker – or what he thought was my locker – to extract the book from my satchel and slink off with it.'

'Instead, he found himself going through my stuff in my locker. That must have thrown him.' I laughed, but quickly sobered. 'Which means I probably saw him come down the final slide while I was waiting for you to catch up with me.'

Hector sat up straighter.

'Do you remember what he looked like?'

'Sorry, not at all. I was too busy looking for you to take any notice of anyone else.'

The bartender, mistaking my outstretched arms earlier as a signal that we were ready to order pudding, strolled over with his order pad in hand.

'Okay, folks, we've got apple crumble, cranachan, or ice cream, or teas and coffees if you prefer.'

I decided instantly. 'Two cranachans, please. Hector, you've just got to try this. It's proper Scottish.'

The bartender gave a lopsided grin as he jotted it down.

'Aye, it is that, dear.'

As he went to fetch our deserts, Hector and I leaned in towards each other, lowering our voices for fear of being overheard.

'There must be something extra special about that particular copy of the book that passed Mr McNab by,' I said. 'Something that also had that guy asking Kate about it back at the shop. How very peculiar that two different people so far apart should be on to it at once. I wonder whether they're working together?'

'Perhaps we'll find out when we take it to the Highland Outdoor Heritage Museum on Friday.' I was looking forward to our visit even more now. 'They might recognise the names on the inscription. Perhaps that's what makes it more valuable.'

'Such as the giver or the recipient being famous people in the history of the Highlands and Islands?' queried Hector. 'Yes, an interesting provenance could add value to an otherwise common or garden book. I always check any second-hand book I acquire for personal inscriptions.'

We sat back to allow the bartender to set down our desserts in front of us. He gave Hector a conspiratorial smile as he turned to go, perhaps assuming Hector was whispering sweet nothings to me. I suppose our physical closeness did make us look rather like a doting couple, rather than amateur sleuths hot on the trail of a mysterious attacker. Actually, we were both. It was a handy disguise.

The situation reminded me of our first dinner date at the fancy Chinese restaurant in Slate Green, almost a year before. We'd just been having a lovely romantic meal when a sudden realisation had forced us to dash off to save someone we barely knew from the vicious intent of a would-be murderer. But now there was a significant difference: it was my lovely Hector who was under attack.

Hector stretched out his legs under the table, touching my calves with the tips of his shoes.

'So if your theory—'

'Our theory,' I corrected him.

'—holds water, we should be home and dry, if you'll excuse the pun, once we're shot of that book.'

I paused to take a mouthful of the delicious mix of porridge oats, whisky and cream, with a handful of late raspberries scattered on top.

'Do we want to be shot of it, if it's so valuable?'

Hector raised his eyebrows. 'I think we do, if it means whoever has possession of it is in danger from this ruthless assailant, whether it's in my satchel or at your parents' house.'

'I think we're safer if it's my parents' house rather than on your person. They still have the burglar alarms and multiple locks on the doors and windows that were installed when the house was a hotel. Not that anyone would know where it was – the attacker might assume you've still got it with you.'

Hector looked down at his cranachan dish.

'Let's decide about whether or not your mum should keep it when we get the experts' verdict on what makes it so special. In the meantime, maybe we'd better play it safe and have a cosy evening in tonight, rather than put ourselves in the path of any further danger.'

'I think that's very sensible, Hector. After all, you've escaped relatively unscathed so far. Your wounds are all superficial. If he has another chance to take a potshot at you, you might not be so lucky.'

I hadn't meant to allude to gunfire; I was speaking figuratively. But if the assailant was so very desperate, there was no guarantee that he wouldn't step up his method of attack and resort to weapons.

Frowning, Hector got up to pay the bill at the bar. The bartender gave him a sympathetic smile. From Hector's expression, he probably assumed I'd just broken up with him.

31

A QUIET EVENING IN

After all the excitement, I was glad to have a cosy evening in with my parents. We had a delicious supper of local wild boar sausages, followed by a game of Scrabble, in which Hector was chuffed to beat the rest of us hollow. Then Hector and I played backgammon, while Mum and Dad played chess.

It was only as Hector and I were drinking cocoa in the kitchen together just before bed that I realised how much more relaxed my parents seemed now, considering only the night before my mum had admitted putting my dad into peril.

'I'm guessing Mum's confessed to Dad too,' I speculated. 'And that he's forgiven her. Did you notice how much more attentive they were being to each other tonight? Then when Dad helped clear the table after supper, he returned the half-full bottle of claret to the kitchen rather than taking it into the sitting room to finish over the course of the evening.'

'Perhaps they've struck a bargain: that he'll stop drinking so much if she stops trying to sabotage his hillwalking.'

We continued the conversation as we were getting undressed ready for bed.

Hector, as usual, was folding his clothes neatly onto a bedside chair while I dropped mine on the floor where I took them off. I slipped on my nightie and clambered into bed.

'I did notice they seemed more physically affectionate this evening then I've seen them so far,' mused Hector. 'They were sitting side by side on the sofa rather than in the usual separate armchairs. I assumed it was just that they were feeling less self-conscious in my presence now that they've got to know me a bit. But perhaps this whole bike business has given a bit of a boost to their love life.'

I held up my hand in protest.

'Please, Hector, say no more. These are my parents we're talking about. Still, I can't tell you how glad I am to see them relaxing in each other's company, and perhaps beginning to resolve the conflict they've been struggling with for so long. They live in such a beautiful part of the country within reach of so many gorgeous places to visit. The Munros are only part of the story. It's a crime that Mum had more or less banned Dad from hillwalking. I mean, it's up to her if she doesn't want to go swimming ever again, but there's no need for Dad to miss out on his favourite hobby too.'

Hector lifted the duvet for me to climb into bed beside him, and I snuggled up against him.

'I think you ought to try again to get her to have counselling,' he said gently, wrapping his arms around me and pulling me closer. 'Whether it's grief counselling, or treatment for post-traumatic stress disorder, it can only help.'

I lay my head on his chest.

'I think you're right. Maybe the incident with the bicycle will make her realise just how out of hand this has all got. From a selfish perspective, I'm glad she never stopped me swimming. She just stopped taking me swimming, which meant I stopped swimming out of doors on the beaches and in the lochs and lochans and burns where we used to go. If I wanted to swim, it had to be where I could get to under my own steam, which basically meant the local public swimming pool; public transport wouldn't get me to our favourite, secret, out-of-the-way places accessible only by car. Still, let's not talk any more about such sadness now. I just hope Mum doesn't let us down at the last minute tomorrow and lose her nerve about coming to the Highland Outdoor Heritage Museum. Instead, let's practise what we've been preaching and make the most of the here and now, shall we?'

With a slow smile, Hector reached for the light switch beside the bed and dimmed the lamp.

32

THE HIGHLAND OUTDOOR HERITAGE MUSEUM

'What strikes me most when I go to places like this is that I'm very glad I live in the twenty-first century,' said Hector as we strolled along the gravel road from the museum's entrance to the northern end of the site in a trailer hauled by a vintage tractor.

We were far away from the city now, and high above it, and surrounded on all sides by beautiful Highland mountain scenery, with swathes of shadowy, ancient forest on all sides.

'Oh, nonsense' I declared. 'You'll soon change your tune when you visit the old-fashioned sweet shop.'

My dad chuckled. 'Which always makes me glad that we live in the age of modern dentistry.'

'But before we do anything else, let's deliver this precious book to the archive office for assessment,' put in Mum. 'After all, that's why we've come here. Then we can relax and spend the rest of the day pottering about the exhibits. There's always something interesting to see, and plenty of re-enactors to help bring history to life for you.'

That was a good idea. I couldn't wait to get this troublesome book out of our hands.

'You'll find it fascinating, Hector,' she continued. 'So many buildings of all kinds, residential, agricultural, commercial, educational, have been shipped here to recreate a detailed record of Highland history and culture. You'll feel like you're travelling through time.'

I was so glad Mum hadn't found an excuse to back out of our trip at the last minute. It was good to see Mum so relaxed and enthusiastic. She was even holding hands with Dad, something I hadn't witnessed for a long time.

The tractor jolted to a halt by a vintage bus stop. We had to wait for the driver to get down from his cab, unlock the door, and lower the steps for us to dismount – a health and safety concession, I suppose, to make sure people couldn't jump on and off while it was moving. As soon as I'd disembarked, my instinct was to head towards the sweet shop, but I followed Mum to the archive office first, as agreed.

The long, low modern office building, with weathered cedar cladding, seemed surprisingly at home among the historic buildings. But Mum's plans were scuppered by a handwritten sign on the door.

'"Office closed due to unforeseen circumstances until 4 p.m."'

'Oh no, not unforeseen circumstances again,' I grumbled.

'Ha!' said Dad. 'Sounds as if the staff are having an unforeseen long lunch, if you ask me.'

Mum shushed him as she handed the book back to Hector, who tucked it inside his satchel.

'Oh well, that gives us plenty of time to see the rest of the site,' she said. 'But we must make sure we're back here for four o'clock. We don't want to miss them, having come all this way.'

For the next couple of hours, we enjoyed wandering around the park, touring an extensive Victorian farmstead, complete with free-range ducks and hens, before heading for an old timber railway station and signal box, furnished with antique enamel signs, old-fashioned ticket office and piles of battered brown leather trunks and suitcases. When we finally reached the sweet shop, tucked behind an old post office, I chose rhubarb and custards, while Hector plumped for humbugs. A lady in a forties dress weighed them out into little white paper bags on a set of cast-iron scales balanced by lead weights.

At the old schoolhouse, we were encouraged by another re-enactor, posing as a strict Victorian schoolmaster, to try our hand at copperplate writing with a dip pen and inkwell. When we stopped for a picnic lunch on the grass outside, my ham sandwich ended up with blue crusts, thanks to my inky fingertips.

The sun came out while Mum was sharing the last of the coffee between our four plastic cups from her big tartan flask. Although the grass was damp, the air felt warm on my face, and I felt more relaxed than I had all holiday, safe in this little time warp of a world.

After lunch, we ambled past an old tin chapel and various workshops, admiring the tools of traditional trades.

'Why is there no old bookshop?' asked Hector, sounding slightly petulant, as we stood in the weaving shed, where Mum was examining the workings of a traditional Harris Tweed loom.

'Perhaps Mum's book will inspire them to start one up in your honour,' I teased, in flippant holiday mood now. 'Every shop's got to start somewhere.'

Mum looked up from the loom.

'Oh, no, I'm thinking they'll want to put it on the kitchen table of a crofter's cottage, or on the pillow of a box bed in a blackhouse. They could put one of those dip pens and inkwells nearby, like we just used in the schoolroom, to make it look as if the inscription was freshly written.'

'Are you up for walking through the forest to the township or do you want to catch the tractor and trailer again?' Dad asked.

'No, let's go on foot and enjoy the scent of the pine forest,' I replied. 'The air's even sweeter up here than it is by the River Ness, away from the traffic and surrounded by all this greenery. Nothing like the elevation of the Munros, though, is it, Dad?'

'A mere three hundred metres,' he replied, 'but enough to make a difference.'

'You can see red squirrels up here, Hector,' I continued. 'They're shy, so you have to keep quiet and look carefully. But they're proper Scottish squirrels, not like the grey ones you get in England. Native British squirrels, like Beatrix Potter's Squirrel Nutkin – so pretty!'

Dad was already striding off ahead, and I ran to catch up with him and linked my arm through his as we entered the woodland path, leaving Hector to stroll behind with Mum. Soon they were chatting comfortably about the revival of the Gaelic language, while Dad and I started a squirrel-spotting contest.

'First one to me!' I breathed, pointing skywards a moment later. 'There it goes, racing along that spindly branch. See?'

'And there!' whispered Dad. 'One all!'

Keeping our voices low so as not to frighten the little creatures, we strolled along with our eyes raised to the treetops, where we were most likely to spot them. They were much shyer than the cheeky grey ones in the Cotswolds.

We skirted the traditional gypsy encampment, wondering, as ever, how anyone could survive a Highland winter with only a tarpaulin tent between them and the elements. Passing the curling pond, we climbed the scrubby footpath that rose above the old sawmill to the hilltop township, a scattering of long, low seventeenth-century Highland cottages, and Hebridean black-houses, built of stone, wood, heather, and moss. A low door led into each dark interior, illuminated only by sparks from smouldering peat fires. As our eyes adjusted to the gloom after the bright, clear sky outdoors, I clung on to Dad, unnerved by the shadows. Anyone could have been hiding in the many recesses – the box bed, the storage loft, the huge wooden chests, the cattle byres.

I glanced behind us, looking for Mum and Hector, but they were nowhere to be seen. Dad noticed me checking for them.

'Knowing your mother, she's probably stopped to read all the information boards along the way,' he suggested. 'Either that or she's giving poor Hector a lesson on the history of curling, whether he wants one or not.'

'Probably,' I agreed. 'I'm sure he won't mind, but I'd better nip back to chivvy them along. I don't want to run out of time before we've seen the township. I think he'll be especially interested in this part because we haven't got anything like it in England.'

'Okay, love, I'll just sit on the bench outside and enjoy the view. It's so peaceful up here. I haven't been out of Inverness with your mum for ages and I want to make the most of it.'

As I began to trudge back down the path, I was almost bowled over by a man in a dark kilt and grubby Harris Tweed jacket ascending at speed. Not the most comfortable kit to go running in, I thought, wondering whether he was a re-enactor late for the start of his shift. In that outfit, he'd have been better suited to the post-war tailor's shop, not up here in the more ancient township. The track was too narrow for us both, so I stood aside on a little grassy hillock to make way for him. As he dashed past, his canvas satchel thumped me on the arm.

'You're welcome,' I said aloud, cross at his failure to thank me or even acknowledge my courtesy.

Only when I came in sight of the curling pond did I realise the reason for his haste. There on the marshy bank was Mum, on her knees, soaking wet, dragging Hector, unconscious, out of the water.

33

UNCURLED

I ran the rest of the way down, and as I sank to my knees beside Mum, Hector's eyelids began to flicker. He too was dripping wet, his dark curls stretched straight by the weight of the murky water and hanging down to touch his shoulders. He must have been completely submerged in the pond to be so sodden.

I grabbed Hector's hands as Mum wiped fronds of pondweed from his face and checked his mouth and nostrils were clear.

'It's okay, he's still breathing,' she said, crouching back on her heels to wipe pondweed from her own face.

'The crucial thing is to get him warm. He wasn't in there long, but the water's cold in the shade of this copse.'

As Hector began to stir, we got on either side of him to raise him into a sitting position. He spluttered, exhaling a mouthful of pond water, then opened his eyes, coughing.

'My satchel!' he cried, casting his hands around on the ground beside him with sudden urgency. 'He did it so as to pinch my satchel.'

Mum glanced at me.

'Oh, dear. It's worse than I thought. He might be concussed. It sounds as if he's delirious.'

As I leaped to my feet, Hector fell against Mum's shoulder, and she put her arm around him to keep him upright.

'No, he's not,' I said. 'He's completely lucid, and I know just what he means.'

'McNab's,' said Hector, brokenly. 'Mr McNab's shoplifter.'

'Look after him, Mum,' I said over my shoulder. 'I'll explain later.'

I sprinted faster than I thought possible back up the steep path, where I found Dad engaging with the man in the kilt, saying something about thatching methods. The man was gazing, wild-eyed, about him, and I realised that Dad must have stopped him to ask a question, assuming he was one of the re-enactors. I guessed the stranger hadn't liked to shake him off for fear of arousing suspicion.

'Dad!' I shouted across the grassy plain between the cottages. 'Dad, stop that man and grab that satchel. It's not his, it's Hector's, and it's got Mum's book in it!'

On hearing me, the kilted man made to run off, but my quick-thinking dad outsmarted him, casually extending his foot to trip him up. The thief fell face down on the springy grass and was silenced by a mouthful of turf. Quick as a flash, Dad strad-dled him and sat on his back, holding his wrists together. As the cuffs of his tweed jacket slid towards his elbows, I recognised a tattoo of a treasure chest that I'd seen once before, on a man in the Inverness swimming pool.

I knelt to unfasten the buckle on the satchel strap, so that I could remove it without Dad having to release any pressure on his arms. The stranger turned his head to watch me rifle through the contents of the satchel.

'Nope, it's not there,' I declared. 'You must have taken it out on your way up and stuffed it in your jacket pocket.' I gulped. 'Or down your kilt.'

Praying that it was the former rather than the latter, I patted down his jacket where I was relieved to find Hector's Gaelic book in the capacious right front pocket.

As I held it aloft in triumph, I realised three other re-enactors, all beshawled women in long, homespun skirts and aprons, had gathered around us. One had a plump, tawny chicken under her arm.

'Do you know him, dearie?' one of them asked me 'Was this laddie troubling you? Shall I call security?'

I considered the prone figure. Clearly he was a stranger to them, and not a member of staff or a volunteer.

'Well, he was, but I don't think he will be any more.'

A strangled voice from the turf. 'Och, I was no'! The lassie's a liar!'

'He most certainly was bothering my friend here,' said Mum, coming across the grass to join us. Hector lagged slightly behind her, still dripping and slightly unsteady on his feet. 'He coshed him on the head with a curling broom, not realising I was nearby. Then he pushed him in the pond and ran off with his bag, leaving Hector out cold and underwater. I dashed over and leaped into the water to haul him out.'

'Oh, dearie me,' said the lady with a chicken under her arm. 'What a good thing he chose the broom and not a curling stone, or the poor laddie would not have a heid left upon his shoulders.'

She set down the chicken, which ran off, squawking, to join its companions, scratching for corn by a blackhouse door. Then she reached beneath her shawl and pulled out a walkie-talkie.

'Sophie, your mum pulled me out of the pond,' Hector said, slumping to his knees on the grass beside me. His voice faltered at first but gained strength as he realised the significance of what had just happened. 'This maniac here hit me on the head and shoved me in the pond. Then your mum dived in to save me. I think I must have blacked out. I... I might have drowned if I'd been on my own.'

'Well, I didn't exactly dive in,' Mum said modestly. 'If I had, you'd have another concussed patient to deal with. That pond's not deep enough for diving. But it's certainly deep enough to drown in. You can drown in a couple of inches of water if you're unconscious.'

She knelt beside Dad and gazed into his eyes.

'Darling, I did it. I got back in the water. That's the first time I've been in the water since...' She didn't need to spell it out. 'I feel like I've just learned to breathe again. Like I haven't breathed for so long.'

She sat back and wrapped her arms around her damp body, pressing the wet fabric against herself as if to preserve the sensation of being immersed. Perhaps she noticed the re-enactor ladies giving her a funny look because she felt the need to explain.

'I've had showers and baths, of course, plenty of those. But swimming? No ponds, no lakes, no lochs, no lochans, no rivers, not even any indoor pools. And oh, how I have missed them!'

She got up and wandered away from us, still hugging herself. Perhaps she needed to be alone to savour the realisation that she was after all still a swimmer.

I glared at the man on the ground.

'All for the sake of a book worth a fiver,' I said. 'Or is it?'

I gave him a quizzical look, hoping he might explain. Then Hector, rallying, leaned back and raised his fist as if about to strike him. I'd never seen Hector so angry. But he let his hand fall to his side, knowing thumping his assailant would not help.

The man twisted his neck to glare over his shoulder at Hector.

'Well, if you wouldn't sell it to me, what else was I to do?'

I gasped. 'You mean you were the guy haranguing Kate to sell you the book back in Wendlebury?'

He spat to dislodge some turf from his mouth.

'Aye, and if you hadn't played so hard to get, it wouldn't have come to this. I think you got off lightly compared to—'

His voice had risen to a yell before he apparently had second thoughts and clammed up, burying his face in the grass again, as Mum returned to stand beside him.

'Compared to what?' I persisted. 'Or rather, to whom? You mean the man you pushed off the boat on the Ness, mistaking him for Hector because he had the same coat and satchel?'

Mum and Dad gasped.

'Sophie!' Mum shrieked. 'You never said!'

'So, what are ye greetin' about? Yon fella's indestructible. He bounces, he floats, and your mammy there made sure he was okay just now. So, tell your crazy daddy there to get off my back, and I'll raise my offer to any price you like for the damn book. I may not be able to pay for it straight away, but if you just give me my book, I'll soon have access to all the money I could wish for.'

'You're the crazy one,' I retorted. 'Like I said, the pesky book's only worth a fiver.'

'It's worth far more than that to me,' said Mum. Hector and I turned to gaze at her. Had she secretly known something about the book that she hadn't told us? 'Because it's the first gift my daughter's boyfriend has given me. And a very thoughtful one too, wasn't it, darling?'

The kilted man turned his head on one side, the more easily to laugh.

'Ha, it'd be wasted on you.' He looked away. 'You don't know the half of it, ye silly old fool,' he said.

Mum drew herself up to her full height.

'Actually, I do. I'm a university lecturer with a special interest in Gaelic language and culture, and the inscription makes it a great social historical interest and value. Why else do you think we've brought it here to the museum? It will be of much greater use where it can be seen by lots of people, rather than just by you.'

At this point, Hector, apparently emboldened by all the practical and moral support Mum had shown him that afternoon, decided to taunt him. 'Besides, it's not even worth a fiver in monetary terms. I picked it up for a pound at a car boot sale. Trust me, I'm a bookseller. I know what I'm talking about.'

'Well, like I said to that old biddy at your shop, I'll pay you fifty quid for it. Surely that's a good enough profit for you?'

'Why on earth would you pay that much for it when the same book sells for a fiver at McNab's?' queried Hector, genuinely puzzled.

'That's none of your business, laddie,' came the rude retort.

'Maybe you should have just accepted his offer, Hector,' I put in. 'If he's daft enough to pay over the odds, that's almost a five-thousand-per-cent mark-up. If you keep that up when you open your second-hand department, you'll soon be able to trade in your Land Rover for a Rolls-Royce!'

'With a chauffeur.' Hector smirked.

'Ha,' said the man. 'I'd get rid of that damned Land Rover too, if I were you, confounding a fellow with your lookalike, posey boy-toy. You said yourself, you're a bookseller, not a gamekeeper.'

'What do you mean, "lookalike"?' Hector paled.

The man turned his face to the turf again, biting his lip, and as he did so, his hands, still in Dad's firm grip, twisted round to expose their palms. I closed my eyes as a chill ran through me.

'Dad,' I said slowly. 'Whatever you do, don't get up. I have a terrible feeling you're sitting on a murderer.'

Before I could explain, reinforcements arrived in response to the re-enactor's radio call for help. I'd been wondering what the museum's security officer would be like. A *Braveheart*-style warrior, face covered in woad and yielding a rough-hewn axe. They turned out to be a pleasant young woman in a green fleece, black jeans and hiking boots on an electric bike. She approached via the path that led up from the curling pond and leaned her vehicle against the wall of the nearest blackhouse. What would its original inhabitants have made of her form of transport?

'Now what have we here?' she said sweetly. 'Is it first aid ye'll be needin' now? As it happens, I'm also the duty first-aider today.'

I looked from Hector to the man on the ground.

'Do you have CCTV on site?' I asked, though it seemed incongruous.

'Aye, dear, we do. We're not entirely true to period on that score.'

'Good. Then I think you might be able to confirm for us that this gentleman beneath my father here just assaulted my boyfriend, pushed him in the curling pond and left him for dead in order to steal his satchel.'

I turned to point at Hector, who was now sitting on the grass with two of the re-enactor ladies patting him dry with their shawls. The third was wringing his damp curls out with her apron. Hector was starting to look much brighter.

'I think it would be best if you all accompany me to the office, and we'll do the necessary down there,' the security officer was saying to the man in the kilt. 'And before you go getting any ideas, sir, there's no point in you trying to make a run for it. You've already caused quite enough trouble. What on earth were ye thinking, near drowning a harmless tourist just so's to thieve a plain old canvas bag?'

'Mr Nicolson to you,' he grunted in a pathetic attempt to assert some dignity. 'And ye don't know the half of it. It's these damn Sassenachs you should be arresting, not me. They're the thieves, taking our precious land and our homes all those years ago.'

She ignored his outburst.

'My fine colleagues over there are going to help you on your way.' She indicated a pair of burly men in woollen breeches and tunics heading towards us from the far corner of the steading. Then she turned to me. 'And I dare say we can find a wee dram in the office for your soggy boyfriend and mammy there, at the very least.'

Mum raised her eyebrows at the mention of Scotch.

'Actually, a nice hot cup of tea all round would probably be for the best,' said Dad, without looking at Mum, 'and perhaps the loan of some dry clothes for my wife and the laddie here.'

34

BRUISED

'All his talk of your lookalike and your Land Rover matching Alasdair's was tantamount to a confession that he was on the scene of his murderer,' I told Hector as we sat in the administration office in the archive building, just after the police had led the man away. 'And he told us outright that he was the man who pestered Kate about buying the book after we'd left Wendlebury.' I paused as the security officer kindly set a tray of tea and biscuits on the low table in front of us. 'But what convinced me that he was Alasdair's killer was the long straight bruise across his right palm. It was precisely compatible with someone who had recently applied force with his hand to a blunt metal instrument with a narrow edge. Like the base of an old-fashioned tyre pump, which is hard enough not to buckle under the rapid repeated pressure of a foot, and therefore strong enough to cause fatal damage to a man's head. And you know how bruising changes colour in the days following a trauma? The bruise on his hand looked a few days old.'

'Yes, a tyre pump could be a murder weapon in the wrong hands,' agreed Dad. 'As that poor man killed at Gretna the other day discovered to his cost. Don't you remember? It was in the paper the other day. They found a tyre pump in the bushes within throwing distance of his body.'

When Mum swooned slightly against his shoulder, he put his arm around her to stop her sliding off her seat.

'Hardly the brightest of killers, if that's the best he can do at hiding his murder weapon,' he continued.

'Stupid enough to use it in the middle of a busy tourist attraction too,' I added.

'On the fringes of one, anyway,' said Hector. 'Right at the edge of the car park, shielded on two sides by the bushes. I suppose he was just lucky that Alasdair chose a relatively secluded spot to park.' He gulped. 'Which I inadvertently made even more secluded when I parked beside him. My goodness, I hope that doesn't make me an accessory to the crime.'

'So that's what he meant by a lookalike?' Dad stared at Hector, wide-eyed. 'The other vehicle mentioned in the article was yours?'

'Sophie Sayers,' said my mum in her best teacher's voice. 'What else have you and Hector not told us?'

Hector and I gazed at each other for a moment, then he gave my hand an encouraging squeeze.

'We'd better tell them everything now, Sophie. They'll find out sooner or later, and it's better to hear the details from us than from the police or from the press.'

My mouth had gone completely dry, and I took a quick swig from my cup of tea before I spoke.

'To be honest, Mum, neither Hector nor I had realised the whole truth until now, but on our way up we stopped at Gretna.'

Before I could get any further, Mum grabbed my left hand and looked anxiously at my empty ring finger. I pulled it back defensively, then relented and took her hand in mine.

'Mum! What do you take me for? I wouldn't get married without inviting you!'

'No, of course not,' she said. 'Besides, I'd have noticed the ring when you arrived.'

'Anyway, when we pulled into the car park, Hector spotted a Land Rover exactly the same as his, and in this weird swarming instinct, he parked beside it, despite it being at the furthest point from the entrance to the visitor centre. It turned out the owner was a fellow bookseller, and we had a pleasant chat with him.'

'The Wigtown bookseller mentioned in the newspaper?' said Dad. 'Or rather, the late Wigtown bookseller, poor soul.'

'Poor man,' said Mum, lowering her eyes. 'What is it about that madman? Has he got a thing against booksellers? I thought you were a harmless enough profession.'

I was glad that Mum designated Hector's chosen career as a profession, and I realised that subconsciously I'd been worrying that as an academic, she might be concerned that I'd hooked up with a shopkeeper. Although he was also an author, and I thought his books were really enjoyable, no one would ever study them at university.

'He picked the wrong bookseller,' explained Hector, paling. 'To be fair, we were both similar in stature, but the other guy, Alasdair, had lots of books on his back seat, and a souvenir sticker from Wigtown on his rear window, so it was an easy mistake to make. Plus, Alasdair had a Scottish accent. From my name, and never having met me, Malcolm Nicolson might have assumed I was Scottish. He had already established by speaking to Kate at my shop that we were heading to Scotland, taking the book with us, and unfortunately, due to the rumour in the village that we were planning to get married at Gretna Green, she told him that would be our destination. It was a false rumour, of course, but enough to put him on our trail.'

'Of course,' echoed Mum, and to my surprise I recognised a trace of disappointment in her voice.

'Although why he went to the trouble of following us all that way, I cannot begin to imagine. He's deluded if he thinks he can sell it at a huge profit, although I can't think of any other way it would make him as rich as he seems to think it would. Anyway, he didn't know what I looked like, so I'm guessing he assumed Alasdair was me. It's all falling into place now. He might have asked Alasdair nicely if he could buy the wretched book, and Alasdair would have kept telling him he didn't have it. If Nicolson assumed Alasdair was me, he would have thought that Alasdair was stonewalling him when he told him he didn't have the book. We didn't realise that when we gave the police our statement at the scene of the crime, and we thought it was just a sad coincidence that the victim was a bookseller. We thought that was the end of it and decided to put it behind us and get on with our holiday. Unfortunately, Nicolson seems to have had other plans.'

'I wonder how long it took him to realise he had attacked the wrong person?' wondered Mum.

'Not that Hector was the right person to attack,' I added quickly, seeing Hector's horrified expression. 'But I'm guessing that after not being able to find the book he was after in Alasdair's Land Rover, he realised he'd killed the wrong bookseller. Then he must have lurked somewhere nearby and followed us up the motorway, realising that it was really Hector who had the book he wanted. If he'd been eavesdropping on our conversation with Alasdair, he will have known that we were heading for Inverness.'

'And that we'd be staying in a house by the riverside,' said Hector, weakly. 'So it was easy enough to follow us in his white van – the same white van that had been hounding us earlier on the motorway.'

'I thought I saw a white van drive past the house while we were parking on the day we arrived,' I put in. 'But Hector convinced me I was imagining it.'

'Well, white vans are pretty ubiquitous,' replied Hector. 'I was only trying to reassure you.'

'And to protect you,' added Dad, ganging up with Hector. I was glad that both Mum and Dad seemed really to have taken to Hector, but if they were going to side with either of us, it surely should have been with me.

'He also will have gathered from our conversation with Alasdair that we'd be visiting McNab's,' I continued. 'He wouldn't have known exactly when, but he might have guessed from Hector's enthusiastic reaction to Alasdair's recommendation that it would be early on in our stay, probably on our first day. He might easily loiter in a big bookshop like that, browsing for days at a time without arousing suspicion, especially when it has a mezzanine that isn't staffed. Old Mr McNab spends most of his day sitting downstairs behind the counter dealing with his customers and working at his computer, and he takes it on trust that no one will pilfer his books or get up to any other mischief.'

'Well, it is in a disused chapel,' put in Mum. 'I should think that makes people think twice about shoplifting when in a former House of God.'

'But not, apparently, about pushing people downstairs,' said Hector, passing his hand over his face.

Dad looked horrified. 'He pushed you downstairs, love?'

'Not me, Dad. Hector.'

'I now realise that must have been a fumbled attempt to lift the book from my jacket pocket,' said Hector. 'Thinking back, I can remember feeling a slight tug somewhere near my waist. Next thing I knew, I was falling down the stairs.'

I gasped. 'Hector, why didn't you tell me that earlier?'

He frowned. 'I didn't want to worry you. Perhaps I was also a bit in denial. Plus, I didn't want to embarrass Mr McNab in front of his customers. I'd hate to be responsible for getting a bookshop closed down for being unsafe.'

I buried my face in my hands. 'Really, Hector?'

Hector brightened. 'At least he didn't get the book. It tumbled down the stairs with me and landed on the floor nearby. I wondered how it had fallen out of my pocket when it was such a tight fit. He must have lifted it but lost his grip on it in the commotion and dropped it down the stairs behind me.'

I picked up the story as Hector drank some tea. 'We know anyone could have guessed we were going to the swimming pool next, because my dry bikini was hanging out of the top of my bag. We think he came after Hector there too.'

'He followed you to the swimming pool?' asked Mum, staring at me in horror.

'Yes, but don't worry, there was no real damage done,' I said hastily. 'He just tried to break into Hector's locker to steal the book.'

Hector clearly disagreed about the nature of the damage done, but thankfully said nothing, presumably to avoid unnerving Mum against swimming again.

'But he broke into my locker by mistake, rather than Hector's, and departed empty handed. What I don't understand, though, is how he knew we were going on that Loch Ness Cruise the next day or coming to the Highland Outdoor Heritage Centre today.'

'He followed you to Loch Ness as well?' Mum's voice was growing fainter.

'Yes, but he got me mixed up with another guy on the boat,' said Hector. 'Someone wearing a similar waxed jacket and carrying the same kind of army surplus satchel. Perhaps he only realised his mistake when he opened the satchel and the book wasn't in it. I doubt the owner ever got his bag back, because he was taken off in an ambulance as soon as we returned to the harbour. Nicolson probably dumped it somewhere.'

'Taken off in an ambulance!' Mum rested her forehead on her hand. 'And there was me thinking you were having a lovely, relaxing holiday. It sounds a complete nightmare.'

'The man was okay though, Mum. He wasn't really hurt. They just took him to hospital as a precaution, probably to cover the cruise company.'

I was careful not to mention that he'd been pushed overboard.

Just then, Hector sneezed. When I reached into my tote bag for some tissues, I was surprised to find the tissue packet felt heavier than a few tissues and a bit of plastic film ought to weigh. I wondered whether a coin had fallen out of my purse and made its way in there somehow. After pulling out a fresh tissue and passing it to Hector, I tipped the packet into the palm of my hand and a small disc of metal about a centimetre deep and two wide fell into my hand. Dad peered across at it.

'If I'm not mistaken, love, that's a tracking device. I've used one occasionally on the hills to give Mum peace of mind in case I got lost and she needed to alert Mountain Rescue.'

'Again,' murmured Mum. Dad waved her comment away.

'They've got a much longer battery life than a mobile phone, because all they do is emit a signal.'

I turned it over in my hand

'Nicolson must have slipped it in there when he raided my

swimming pool locker,' I realised. 'I can't remember using the tissues since then, which is why I didn't notice it before.'

Mum took a deep breath. 'Is there anything else you two haven't told me?'

I gave a sheepish grin. 'Isn't that enough for one day?'

'I'd prefer a straight no, darling, if it could be arranged.'

I laughed.

'Sorry, Mum. Those are all the confessions I have for you for now. But what we still have to solve is why Malcolm Nicolson wanted your little book so much that he was prepared to commit murder to get it.'

'Perhaps we'd better write down everything you know so far when we get home and then something might leap out at us as the missing piece of the puzzle,' said Dad. 'Also it will save time when we go to the police station in Inverness tomorrow to make our statements.'

I was glad the police had taken pity on Mum and Hector's sodden state and allowed them to recover and change their clothes before going to the police station in Inverness to give our side of the story next day.

Dad drained his cup.

'Now, if you've all finished your tea, we'd better start making a move homewards.'

'Good thing you were on the ball, Sophie,' said Hector as we climbed into Dad's car for the journey back home. 'Or our lunatic friend might have got off with a simple charge of assault for what he did to me today. I'm glad we have some thinking time now to piece the whole story together.'

As Dad reversed out of our parking space, a plain white van in the far corner of the parking lot caught my eye. Stuck across the windscreen was a large strip of black and yellow tape bearing the words, 'Police aware'.

35

SOMETHING FISHY

We must have been a strange sight as we headed home, Mum in the front passenger seat in a rough brown woollen dress and shawl, and Hector beside me on the back seat in tweed breeches, woollen cloak and high boots.

'I suppose it could have been a lot worse,' said Hector as we joined the A9. 'He might have accosted me in the sawmill beside the curling pond.'

The thought of rusting tools and serrated blades sent a chill right through me as I pictured Hector as James Bond, tied to a saw bench with a rotating blade headed towards him. I laid a hand on his tweedy thigh, the rough fabric prickling my fingers.

'What a lot we've been through, all for the sake of a worthless book,' I said in a small voice.

'Only a dip in a pond for me,' said Mum dreamily from the front seat. 'Which is hardly cause for complaint. Which reminds me, darling.' She turned to Dad. 'You were talking about taking Hector up the Cuillins. When you do, Sophie and I could come with you and go swimming in the Fairy Pools.'

'Fairy Pools?' echoed Hector. 'What's that, some Highland fantasy-themed water park?'

The rest of us laughed.

'No, silly. It's the name of a natural water feature on Skye, and although they're popular with tourists, they're still quite unspoiled. But they're well named because they are pretty magical, aren't they, Mum?'

Mum nodded. 'Yes, love, and I'll be glad to be reminded of just how magical they are all over again. You know, I feel like a new woman after my little dip in the curling pond just now. Swimming just resets me somehow. '

It would be a very welcome break, especially now that we knew we'd no longer have a dangerous madman on our tail.

Mum bought fresh local fish for tea on the way home, which I took as another sign that she was beginning to embrace her inner mermaid again.

'One thing I'm not clear on still is why the book was so important to him?' Dad asked as we sat down to dinner that night. 'I mean, he doesn't strike me as a historian or a collector of old books.'

Mum set a dish of gleaming poached salmon at the centre of the table.

'Nor a reformed, lapsed Christian with a sudden urge to read a book of religious poetry,' said Hector. 'But he seemed to think the book was worth a fortune, when its market value is negligible. Why would anyone commit murder for the sake of it when he could easily have bought the same edition for a fiver? It's hard to believe anyone could be so callous.'

'Sentimental value?' I suggested. 'Because the older Malcolm Nicolson had died, and he wanted it as a tender memento of his father?'

'Ha! He doesn't strike me as the sentimental type, and

besides, it was hardly an inscription overflowing with paternal love,' said Hector. 'I'm guessing that scolding inscription is what made him get rid of the book in the first instance, before he realised its true value. Assuming, of course, that the inscription was to him, although equally it could have been to an earlier ancestor than his father whose name was handed down the family line to him. There's no date on it to tell us for sure, but either way, he's the sort of ignoramus who would throw a book in a dustbin to get rid of it rather than finding it a good home.'

'But that wouldn't account for how it reached Clevedon,' I observed.

'No, he could have sold the books as a job lot to a local second-hand book dealer, before he realised the true value of this particular book,' said Hector. 'Quite how he realised its worth, we don't yet know. But perhaps another relation knew about it and asked him what had happened to it, and it was only then that he realised he'd inadvertently disposed of something valuable. The dealer might have shipped any books that weren't suitable for their shop to that firm down in Somerset, near my parents. You know the one, Sophie: Books by the Shelf. It sells books en masse to places that need to fill bookshelves for cosmetic purposes. Hotels and pub chains often want instant libraries to furnish their premises. Film sets and theatres need them too, as do antique shops. The stall I bought it from at that car boot sale is run by the wife of the firm's owner, and she always has a box of oddments that have lain on their shelves unused for more than a certain amount of time but that have a curiosity value. Maybe no-one had ever asked them for books in Gaelic, which is why she took that particular book to her stall at the car boot sale. She's a friend of my mum's, and she often alerts Mum to interesting books for my curiosity collection. That's where I got my copy of *The*

Adventures of Sherlock Holmes in Pitman shorthand, for example.'

'Oh yes, I love that book!' I cried. 'It makes me want to learn Pitman shorthand just so that I can read it!'

'It's not as if the inscription has any obvious financial implications,' said Mum. 'I think he would have had a valid claim to that in any case as next in line. The inscription is just tearing him off a strip for his behaviour.'

'No wonder he got shot of it,' said Dad. 'I wonder which dealer he sold it to?'

'I'm not sure whether there are on any on Lewis and Harris,' added Mum. 'So I'm guessing he got in a house clearance service to get rid of his late father's possessions.'

I swallowed.

'What if the house clearance company sold all his valuable books to Alasdair? If Nicolson knew, his attack on Alasdair might not have been a case of mistaken identity, but a purposeful act of vengeance for getting rid of what he discovered too late was the key to a fortune. It could just be a coincidence that he came upon Alasdair as he was talking to us, and that we had the book he was after, which Alasdair couldn't possibly have known, unless we'd told him. My goodness, Hector, I think you recognised that subconsciously. Do you remember, the other day you were saying you wished you'd shown Alasdair Mum's book, but you didn't quite know why? We know now it might have saved his life. If we'd sold Nicolson the book, he'd have left Alasdair alone. Of course, whether we'd have sold it to him or not is another matter. After all, you did buy it for Mum.'

Hector raised a hand.

'Hang on a minute, Sophie, that doesn't work. If they'd sold all Nicolson's books to Alasdair, Nicolson would have just

contacted him at his shop in Wigtown, not ambushed him in
Gretna. Also, we know he tried to buy the book at my shop. No, I
think it was just a chance meeting with Alasdair and a genuine
case of mistaken identity. He'd followed a bookseller in a Land
Rover from the Cotswolds, and when he saw two Land Rovers
parked together, one with a back seat full of valuable old books,
he assumed that was the one he'd been following and that Alasdair, its driver, was the proprietor of Hector's House. We'd
shaken him off on the motorway when his engine overheated, so
he would have only reached Gretna a little while after us, once
we'd already parked and gone inside the visitor centre. Perhaps
Nicolson will tell the police in his statement how that came
about, and I'm not sure we need spend any more time on that
ourselves. What's more important – and less likely for the police
to find out – is how that book is the key to a fortune. If we knew
that, everything else might start to make more sense. We must
make sure he doesn't profit by his crimes.'

'Perhaps we can work it out between us,' I said hopefully.
'Are there hidden clues in the inscription, like some kind of
code? That's the only feature that seems to distinguish it from
the other editions readily available in Mr McNab's stock, and
presumably in other second-hand bookshops all over Scotland –
maybe even poor Alasdair's too – so that must hold the answer.'

'Could be, darling,' said Mum. 'But it's not as if the inscription has legal implications, like a last will and testament, leaving
his father's croft to him. The ownership of crofts is highly prized,
even though it's a real challenge these days to make a living from
them. Most successful crofters run small businesses or have
multiple jobs to stay afloat. I can't picture Malcolm Nicolson
being that hard-working, given the strength of his father's invec-
tive against him.'

'Perhaps the book itself is the key to a secret code,' I suggested.

Hector perked up. 'Like the copy of Lamb's *Tales from Shakespeare* that Jim Wormold uses in Graham Greene's *Our Man in Havana* to send coded messages back to his control in London?' Then his face fell. 'No, that wouldn't work. Correspondents just need to possess the same edition of a book so that the references tally. It wouldn't work with a one-off inscription in one copy. So, if that was the secret, Nicolson could equally have used any of McNab's copies, provided there were identical editions.'

Hector pursed his lips.

'I think we'd better examine the book more closely to see what clues it might yield.'

36

THE SECRET WITHIN

'Perhaps the inscription isn't the only distinguishing feature,' I continued. 'What's more, if it's so valuable to him, maybe it could be valuable to us too.'

'What, you mean something like there being diamonds hidden inside its spine?' Dad suggested, laughing. 'Or the combination to a safe full of Nazi gold held in a Swiss vault.'

'Or a treasure map hidden inside it,' said Hector. 'Or a message in invisible ink.'

'That could be fun,' put in Dad. 'I quite fancy going digging for buried treasure.'

'Seriously, though, perhaps he is some sort of modern pirate,' said Mum.

'That sounds more likely than being a secret agent,' added Dad. 'That was going to be my next line of enquiry. That he'd mistaken poor Alasdair for some kind of foreign spy and had bumped him off as part of a Soviet plot to undermine the government.'

'Maybe the book contains secret instructions that are the key to a drug-smuggling business,' put in Hector. 'Drop-off and pick-up points, for example. That seems more likely than a treasure map. You never hear of anyone digging up buried treasure these days.'

I raised my forefinger to object. 'What about metal detectorists? Or builders and farmers finding Roman or Viking remains when they're turning over new ground? There are often stories like that in the news.'

I helped myself to some more salmon.

'Maybe in wilder, less inhabited parts of the Highlands and Islands, detectorists might still find historic treasure tucked away somewhere. In some of the remoter hamlets and farms, there aren't many passers-by, and if anyone found something, it would be easy to keep it a secret. They wouldn't necessarily alert the press to get their picture in the paper or post it all over social media. If it happened to me, I wouldn't want all that public attention.'

'You'd tell the tax man, though, wouldn't you, love?' asked Dad. 'Don't forget the rules of Treasure Trove. Your findings might count as belonging to the nation or to the Crown, although you might get to keep some of it, or be rewarded financially for your efforts.'

I suppressed a smile. 'Yes, of course, Dad.' Dad was very hot on tax, having handled all the details of Auntie May's will and still managed the royalties that would continue to accrue for seventy years after her death. I supposed that task will fall to me when he's gone. I'd never really thought of that before.

'It's like the old joke, love – if you want to win the lottery, you have to buy a ticket.'

I'd just taken a sip from my wine glass and nearly choked on it.

'That's it!' I cried, sitting, setting my glass down so fast that a little tidal wave of Pinot Grigio surged out onto the tablecloth. 'I bet he was after a winning lottery ticket. I bet there's a winning lottery ticket tucked inside the book that someone's used as a bookmark, then mislaid the book without checking the numbers, then got rid of it before they'd realised they'd hit the jackpot. Doesn't the inscription include gambling in its list of things the signatory is railing against? No wonder Nicolson was in such a desperate rush to get it back. Lottery tickets have a claim-by date. He needed to redeem it before it became just a worthless piece of paper. Like Cinderella having to get home before midnight struck and her clothes turned back into rags.'

Mum clapped her hands in applause, before Hector groaned in disappointment.

'I'm sorry, sweetheart, that's a great theory, but I'm afraid it can't be right, because I bought the book in January. In the National Lottery, you have to claim your winnings within a hundred and eighty days of the draw, otherwise your prize money just goes back into the pot and is lost to you forever.'

I slumped back in my chair, disappointed, then immediately sat up straighter.

'That may be true of the National Lottery, but that's just one type of lotto. Others are available. Maybe there's another scheme that has a longer period for claims. Hector, where did you put that pesky book? Let's check it out now so that we know for sure.'

Hector got up from the table and went out into the hall, where he had hung his satchel on a peg. He brought the satchel back into the dining room and extracted the book. After setting the bag on the floor, he opened the book at the front endpapers and began turning the pages over carefully, one by one, until he reached the end. We all watched, breathlessly, letting our food grow cold.

'No, it's a wild goose chase, I'm afraid,' he said as he reached the back endpapers.

I reached across the table to tap the back inside cover.

'No, it's not. Look, I can see from here that there's something under the back endpaper. Look, it's bulging a bit, and it's thicker than the one at the front. It's raised up, as if someone's peeled it off the cover, stuck something underneath it, and stuck it down again.'

Hector laid the book flat on the table and ran his finger over the back endpaper. There was a distinct bulge.

Dad delved into his trouser pocket to produce his multi-bladed penknife designed for hillwalkers. He selected a slim blade and pulled it out before setting it down within Hector's reach.

'Here. This should slip through it easily.'

'No!' cried Hector and Mum together.

'That would be vandalism in such a beautiful book,' added Hector.

'My book!' said Mum, snatching it up and hugging it to her chest.

'Sorry, love, but if we're to get to the bottom of this, I think we'd better steam it open,' suggested Dad, gently prising her clenched fingers from the book. 'I'll put the kettle on right now. Come and join me when you've finished eating.'

We deserved to get indigestion for the speed with which we polished off our meal, before dashing out to the kitchen. Dad was holding the book in oven gloves as he directed the steam from the kettle at the inside back cover until the glue on the end paper began to melt and the page curled away from the board.

We all gathered around the kitchen table as he carefully lifted the end paper free of the back cover board. Beneath the patterned sheet lay a single piece of paper the size of an old-fashioned bus ticket. On it were two strings of six figure numbers, a decimal point after the first one.

'A telephone number without the area code?' Mum suggested. 'Shall we phone it and see who answers?'

'But how would you know which area code to use?' asked Dad.

Mum considered for a moment. 'I could work my way through the codes for the most likely areas to have been the source of an inscription like this. I'd start with the Western Isles, as that seems to be most likely.'

I had another idea.

'Hang on, maybe it's the combination for a safe. Perhaps he inherited the safe but not the code. He now needs the code to access his fortune, and only found out where it was hidden after he'd disposed of the book.'

'Wait a minute,' said Hector, who with the instincts of a bookseller was now pressing down the end paper to try to restore the book to its former condition. 'Look, there's another message on the very last page. It's very faint, in pencil, which is why we missed it earlier. It shows up a bit darker now that we've dampened the page with steam. It's in Gaelic again. Shona, can you do the honours, please?'

He passed the book to Mum, who read it aloud with her perfect Gaelic accent, then translated it. 'It means: "If you've read this far, you deserve what you'll find beneath this spot, and if you haven't, serve you right." It sounds rather more poetic in the original. But no mention of a safe. So perhaps it's not a combination after all. What else would you use a series of six numbers for. A password for a computer or phone?'

'I'm guessing the old boy who wrote the inscription wouldn't have been *au fait* with IT,' said Dad. 'Presumably Nicolson's grandfather or father, as it's written with a ballpoint pen rather than a dip pen or fountain pen. Ballpoints were invented by László Bíró just before the start of the Second World War, so that makes the inscription quite recent. Although perhaps I'm being unduly ageist. So, what do we do now? Do we tell the police to tell Nicolson we've found the numbers hidden in the book to see his reaction? Perhaps the shock of it will make him confess. I admit I'd quite like to know the answer to this mystery, although I'd prefer we'd solved it ourselves rather than having to ask him to tell us.'

'What, and allow him to profit by a crime?' cried Mum. 'Not likely!'

Hector passed his hand over his curls, which had quickly sprung back to their original form once he'd showered out the pond water on returning home.

Dad got up from the table to refill and turn on the kettle for our after-dinner coffee.

'Oh well, let's sleep on it. Maybe when we go into the police station tomorrow to make our official statements, they'll have found out more about him, including facts we couldn't possibly have guessed. I take it you're going to press charges for assault, Hector?'

Hector rubbed his nose.

'If I had only myself to think about it, and he hadn't murdered poor Alasdair, I'd be tempted to drop it as we live so far away. It would mean leaving the shop for longer if it goes to trial, and we have to give evidence, and so forth. We could end up having to stay here for ages if the trial is protracted, and that wouldn't be good for my business.'

I shot him a reproachful look. But for the grace of God – and Mum's brave rescue of him – Hector could have been Nicolson's second murder victim.

'But it's the least I can do in Alasdair's memory to make sure

Nicolson is charged for all his attacks. Besides, a man that irra-
tional may well have left a trail of other crimes in his wake. The
longer he's kept away from society, the better.'

'Let's talk about it in the morning,' I suggested, wanting to
suspend the discussion until we were out of my parents' earshot
and could talk in detail about the previous attacks.

Dad sighed as he spooned ground coffee into the cafetiere.

'I suppose this trip to the police station in the morning will
scupper our hillwalking trip to Skye, and your trip to the Fairy
Pools, love. Still, I always say it's good to leave something
undone whenever you visit a place, to give you an excuse to
return. The Munros will still be there for us next time you come
up north, Hector, for reasons of pleasure, rather than for the
purposes of the court. I hope you won't keep me waiting too
long. I'd already got my Ordnance Survey map out for the
Cuillins.'

Hector glanced at Mum, who, to my relief, nodded her
approval for the trip.

I clapped my hand to my mouth. 'Dad, you've hit it! That's it!
Those six figures. They're geographical bearings. Aren't those
always a string of six figures?'

Dad poured hot water onto the coffee grounds and set the
cafetiere on the kitchen table.

'Yes, that's right. Well, two pairs of six figures, anyway. Wait,
what were the numbers again? Where's that scrap of paper? Let
me see them.'

For safekeeping, Hector had placed it in the middle of the
book as if it were a bookmark, and he pulled it out now to show
to Dad.

'Hmm, those numbers sound familiar,' said Dad. 'I think
they'll pinpoint somewhere in the Western Isles. Maybe not
Lewis and Harris, but one of the smaller ones to the south,

Barra, or Benbecula or North or South Uist or Mingulay. There are plenty of possibilities. I can soon find out exactly which one.' He pulled his phone out of his pocket and opened an app he uses for planning his hillwalking trips. 'The Western Isles are another name for the Outer Hebrides,' I reminded Hector, pushing down the plunger on the cafetiere. 'You know, Lewis and Harris and so forth.'

Mum fetched coffee cups and saucers from the cupboard and cream from the fridge.

Dad looked up from his phone. 'Yes, it's a tiny uninhabited island to the west of Benbecula. Sophie, love, I think you might not be far off the mark with your treasure map theory. I think there must be something of value on this little strip of land, which, to any uninformed onlooker would look worthless, other than perhaps for summer grazing.'

Mum sat back heavily in the seat.

'The Laird's Gold,' she breathed. 'I bet you anything it's the Laird's Gold.'

37

THE MISSING LINK

Mum took a deep breath before telling us the story of the Laird's Gold.

'There was a myth that during the Highland Clearances, a daring Highlander broke into the home of a hated landlord and escaped with a great hoard of gold jewellery that was never found again. He went into hiding, sheltered by fellow Highlanders who saw his act as fair revenge for the theft of their land and their livelihood. They may also have hoped for a share of the spoils as their reward.' She paused to take a sip of wine. 'Of course, they'd never have been able to sell it and realise its worth because it would have been obvious that it was stolen property and whoever presented it would be taken to be a thief and hanged for it. There was a rumour it had somehow been smuggled overseas by one of the many displaced crofters forced to emigrate to survive, and that it would pitch up in colonial Canada or Australia years later. There's still a huge bond between the descendants of those settlers.' She paused for thought. 'But there was also a rumour that it had been concealed somewhere in Scotland and then lost, perhaps in a sea cave, washed away by a freak tide. There's also a theory that the thief had been killed or died unexpectedly before he could pass the secret on, so that the whereabouts of its hiding place might be lost forever. Or that the secret would be handed down the generations until the hated landlords had been vanquished and the gold could be reclaimed and sold without fear of retribution. What was that daring Highlander's name? Oh yes, I remember now: Calum MacNicol.'

I only realised I've been holding my breath when I let out a huge exhalation in disappointment.

'Sorry, Mum, that can't be the solution. There's no mention of a Calum MacNicol in the inscription. It's signed to and from Malcolm Nicolson.'

Mum covered her mouth with her hands.

'But that's not a different name at all. I've just realised, it may be Gaelic version of the same name. Gordon, quick, do a search on your phone.'

We held our breath while Dad looked it up, then nodded, wide-eyed.

'Can it really be possible that Malcolm Nicolson is the descendant of the infamous Calum MacNicol, and these coordinates show the location of the Laird's Gold?'

We gazed at each other in silence for a moment.

'That holier-than-thou inscription in the front of the book might even be a smokescreen,' I suggested. 'And the Malcolm Nicolson who wrote it might be as big a rogue as Malcolm the Murderer.'

'Or perhaps he was still uncomfortable at the thought of profiting from crime and left it partly to chance whether Malcolm the Murderer might read it,' said Mum. 'Perhaps he trusted to fate – or to God, as it's devotional poetry – to deliver the treasure to Malcolm only if he read the book to the end. If not, fate or God, or whatever you want to call it, would have made its decision clear: Malcolm didn't deserve it.'

'How awful that Alasdair had to die in the process, though,' I said, my eyes filling with tears.

'The plundered gold would be worth a fortune, if he managed to dig it up and sell it now,' said Mum. 'At least, if he was allowed to keep it, which would be questionable.' She put her hand to her mouth. 'So when the elder Nicolson wrote in the inscription that the book would make him richer, he didn't mean spiritually at all, as I presumed earlier, but literally.'

I grimaced. 'I suppose Malcolm might have planned to melt the gold down to avoid detection and sell it as plain gold. He seemed sufficiently ruthless and desperate. Not your typical historian, keen to preserve ancient artefacts.'

'If our theory is correct, at least the treasure is safe where it is for now,' said Mum. 'He can't dig it up without knowing the precise location, and I'm not about to tell him.'

Dad winked at Hector.

'What about it, son? Fancy coming with me on a treasure-hunting expedition?'

Mum coughed.

'That's not funny, darling. If this information enables it to be retrieved, it must go either to the descendants of the landlord it was stolen from or to a museum. Obviously, I'd prefer the latter. We must take the book to the police station as evidence, and it will be down to them to pursue the treasure and reunite it with its rightful owner – the descendants of the laird from whom it was stolen during the Highland Clearances. But it would be a good idea if we also take with us some background information on the Laird's Gold, to point them in the right direction. I don't suppose they come across this kind of crime every day, with its roots in distant history.'

'It's a pity we're so honest,' said Dad, with a twinkle in his eye. 'Otherwise we could jump in a boat with a spade and dig the treasure up ourselves. Just think of it, Shona; we could be rich!'

Mum shook her head to admonish him.

'I'd rather be honest,' said Mum. 'Now, after all the excitement, I think we could all do with an early night. We'll have a difficult morning tomorrow when we go to make our statements at the police station.'

None of us disagreed.

38

THE LAST DAY

'It's unfortunate that yesterday's shenanigans put paid to my hopes that we might spend today on Skye,' said Dad as we left Inverness police station around noon next day. 'That's a shame. I was looking forward to showing Hector one of his namesakes.'

'And I was looking forward to swimming in Fairy Pools again with Mum.'

I slipped my arm through hers as we strode back to the car park. I hoped this delay wasn't going to give her time to invent an excuse to renege on her vow to get back into open water swimming.

'Never mind, darling, we'll do that next time you come home,' she said, patting my hand. 'Only don't leave it so long next time.'

'We won't,' I said, fixing Hector with a meaningful look.

'I wouldn't tackle the Cuillins in winter months, son, but maybe we can do them next spring once the days are getting longer,' said Dad.

Hector smiled. 'I'll look forward to that.'

'And I'll make sure I put in plenty of swimming training at

Slate Green pool in the meantime, to build my swimming muscles back up,' I added. 'I might even teach you to swim too, Hector.'

Hector didn't miss a beat. 'And in return I'll teach you to drive, sweetheart.'

I was taken aback.

'Oh,' I said. 'Okay.'

'We've witnesses, mind!' He pointed at Mum and Dad.

'It sounds as if you'd both do well out of that deal,' said Dad. 'Now, Mum and I really must get off to work. I've a seminar to teach this afternoon.'

'And I've a PhD student to supervise,' added Mum. 'But as it's your last night here, you can spend the afternoon packing, and Dad and I will make sure we're home as soon as we can for a nice family dinner so that you can have an early night before your long drive tomorrow.'

'We'd like to leave at first light tomorrow so we can get all the way home in daylight.'

'Good idea, son,' said Dad. 'That's what I'd do, if I were you.'

To my surprise and delight, Mum didn't add a single word of warning.

'This week's gone too quick, Mum,' I said, giving her a long, tight hug. 'Perhaps you can come and see us sometime soon. You get far more holiday than I do.'

'You want to have a word with that boss of yours, love,' said Dad with a wink. 'I think he's working you too hard.'

'I take good care of her, really,' replied Hector.

'I know you do, son. It's good to see her so happy.'

Hector gazed at me fondly.

'If she's still smiling despite all we've been through this week, I must be doing something right.'

'An awful lot, right, if you ask me,' said Mum. 'Anyway, Loch

Ness and the Munros will still be here, whenever you return, and so will the Fairy Pools.'

I pointed to a couple of ducks on the river to distract everyone from the tears of happiness and relief that were welling up in my eyes.

39

PARTNERS IN CRIME

'Bye bye, Gretna Green,' said Hector as we drove past its turn-off, 'and I don't mind if I never see you again.' He reached for my hand. 'Don't worry, that's got nothing to do with its historic associations. It's just that I've other plans for where to break our journey on the way home.'

'Please tell me it's not another tourist visitor centre,' I said, 'I've rather lost my appetite for places like that after our journey up.'

He squeezed my hand in reassurance.

'So, where is it, then?' I asked, wriggling in my seat.

'Wait and see.'

He made me wait until we were over halfway home, when he turned off at the motorway junction for the seaside town of Morecambe and followed the signs to the seafront. We found a parking space on the promenade and leaped down from our seats, glad for the chance to stretch our limbs and our backs after such a long drive.

Hector caught my hand, and we began to stroll along the

promenade, admiring the Lakeland Fells rising above the far side of the horseshoe-shaped bay.

'Now, sweetheart, those are definitely not Munros,' he told me solemnly, and I laughed.

'You're learning,' I replied.

We strode on until we reached the famous statue of the old comedian from the days of black and white television who had taken his stage name from the town of his birth. Hector looked up at the jovial figure on the plinth above us.

'My mum and dad still rave about him and his old comedy partner Ernie Wise,' he said. 'Apparently their show was the highlight of their weekly viewing when they were at school. Dad reckons their comedy partnership is second only to Laurel and Hardy's, and that's why I thought I choose this place to ask you my important question. Actually, I'd have taken you to see the Stan Laurel statue, since we watched that Laurel and Hardy film earlier this week, but it's too far off our route to be practical, on the east coast, near Newcastle-upon-Tyne.'

He turned to take both my hands

'You want us to go into comedy?' I laughed at the ridiculous thought. "Which of us do you propose as a straight man? Bagsy not me!'

Hector laughed.

'I'm talking about quite a different kind of partnership, sweetheart. In this last year, you have made such a difference to Hector's House as a business. Not just by providing alluring company for your esteemed employer. You've had endless ideas to help me improve the business. You've turned the tearoom into a destination in its own right, and you've supported and encouraged me to expand and develop the business. I'd rather allowed it to stagnate or at least to plateau before you came along. In fact, if it wasn't for your input, I might not even still be in business.'

'But what about your books?' I put in. 'You've been subsidising your shop's income with your writing, so that you don't have to draw a proper salary out of the shop's profits. That's all down to you. I can't take any credit for that.'

He brushed my objection aside.

'I'd be doing that anyway. You see, I've never told you this before – perhaps I've never even admitted it to myself – but I really enjoy writing romantic novels. I'd keep writing them even if readers stopped buying them. I admit that wasn't why I took it up at first. I just needed an extra income. I love it now that I'm in the flow, and I get a buzz out of making readers happy. But I want to be a bookseller too, and I've realised after the last few days just how much you've done to make it possible for me to keep living both dreams.'

I pulled my hands free of his and threw myself at him in a heartfelt hug. This was all the acknowledgment I secretly craved. But there was more to come.

'So, the thing is, Sophie,' he was saying into my ear as he hugged me close and stroked my hair, 'I'd like to make you an equal partner in the business.'

He leaned back to judge my expression.

'No, that's too much,' I was about to say. But then I realised that it wasn't. It was just right. And although I'd been sad to say goodbye to my parents and leave the fresh Highland air and the buzz of Inverness behind me, now I couldn't wait to get home to Wendlebury and see what the future would bring to Hector's House, and to Hector and me.

40

CLOSING MUSIC

Hector had one surprise left for me. As we arrived back in the village in the early evening and drove along the High Street, everything seemed familiar, but a little different too. Or perhaps it was just me that had changed. My perspective on Wendlebury life had shifted a fraction now that I felt I had a more permanent and significant role at Hector's House. We had been away less than a week, but it felt like very much longer.

As we reached the bookshop, instead of turning into his usual parking space beside the shop, Hector stopped on the main road, pulled on the handbrake and turned off the ignition. When I opened the door and jumped down onto the pavement, I understood the reason why.

Gruff swearing, accompanied by higher pitched expletives and a strange musical clatter, were emanating from the direction of the front door to his flat which opened at the side of the shop. We marched round to seek out the source of the noise and found Billy, bent over almost backwards, beneath a gleaming white upright piano. From the barrage of shrill swear words halfway up the stairwell, I gathered Tommy was at the other end of the instrument.

When Hector rushed forward and relieved Billy of his load, the old man put out one hand to steady himself on my shoulder, while with the other wiping his damp brow with a grubby hanky.

'For goodness' sake, Billy, I didn't mean you to move it.' Hector had to shout to be heard over the jangling of the piano keys. 'That's it, Tommy, to you, one step at a time.'

Billy waited to catch his breath before he replied. 'No, but the lads who brought it were complaining about having to work on a Sunday, and they offered me and the boy here twenty pounds to get it up the stairs for you so they could get off home quicker.'

Hector growled in a combination of anger and extreme physical effort. I guessed he had the heavy end.

'I'll be having words with that delivery service on Monday for taking advantage of an old man.'

Billy raised his eyebrows.

'Actually, I thought I was rather taking advantage of them. But as you like.'

Billy shouted round the corner to Tommy. 'You'll have to be a bit quicker if you want your five quid before I get off to the Bluebird, son.'

Tommy grunted in agreement as a final thump indicated the piano had made it as far as the landing. A moment later came the far lighter sound of Tommy scampering down the stairs. He jumped down the last two steps, swinging both arms for forward propulsion, and landed in front of Billy, his hand outstretched for his fiver.

'Thanks, Bill,' he said. His friend dropped five one-pound

coins into his palm, and Tommy clenched his fist around them straight away, as if fearing they might escape.

'So, is this piano for your wedding party, miss?' Tommy sounded hopeful. 'If you need a waiter to help you, you could hire me if you like. I could pass round the drinks and snacks on a silver tray. I'd be good at that.'

He held up one hand on a level with his shoulder, palm upwards, miming an accomplished sommelier. The prospect of putting Tommy in charge of a tray of glasses of wine filled me with dread.

'Once and for all, Tommy, Hector and I haven't got married.'

Tommy shrugged.

'Why, was that Grunt and Groan place shut when you got there? Bad luck. That's what you get for not getting married here at St Bride's where all your mates are. Still, my sister will be pleased. That means she's still in with a chance of being your bridesmaid. If it's the cost that's holding you back, don't worry. She could use the same dress that she's wearing for Carol and Ted's wedding.'

'What? Since when have Carol and Ted been engaged?'

But Tommy was already off down the street, rattling his earnings between his palms and whistling cheerfully.

'Since the day after you left for Scotland,' said a familiar voice behind me. 'Hello, Sophie! Welcome home! Good trip?'

Kate had come out of the shop to greet us. Although Hector's House isn't open on a Sunday, she told me Hector had texted, asking her to drop by to supervise the arrival of a special delivery, due to take place before we got back from Scotland. Unfortunately, she'd reached the shop only after the delivery van had left.

'So, it's not just another village rumour?'

'True, as I stand here, Sophie. Actually, there's a rather sweet story behind it, and it's all down to you.'

She put an arm around my shoulders to lead me into the shop, perhaps realising she was in dereliction of duty. We headed for the tearoom counter, which I beamed at as if greeting an old friend.

Kate and I sat down at an empty table.

'Apparently it was Carol who popped the question,' she began to explain. 'When Ted heard Carol advising you not to elope to Gretna Green, he panicked, thinking she was anti-marriage and that she'd had enough of him too. Of course, we know she's not anti-marriage. She just didn't want you to repeat the mistake she'd made in her youth. That's why Ted applied to do temporary cover here while you were away, to give her some space while he thought about what to do next. Then it was Carol's turn to panic. Presumably frightened that she was losing him, she was bold enough to ask him to marry her, thinking it would be a case of kill or cure.'

'Go, Carol!' I found myself beaming. 'I don't suppose her proposal met with any resistance. Ted's besotted with her. How lovely!'

Kate returned my smile.

'Yes, it's a while since we've had a village wedding. Now there's something nice to look forward to as the weather turns cold and the days shorter and darker.'

Hearing the opening bars of 'Für Elise' from above our heads, I jumped to my feet.

'Now, if you'll excuse me, Kate, I need to go and find out why there's now a piano in Hector's flat. Thank you so much for keeping an eye on our shop while we've been away.' Our shop. It sounded so good.

Despite the ache in my legs after sitting still for so long on our journey home, a surge of excitement at the prospect of trying out a beautiful instrument gave me the strength to bound up the stairs two at a time.

Hector had pushed the piano against the wall to the right of the front window, having moved a side table to make room for it.

'There.' He stood back to admire the effect of his new acquisition before placing the side table to serve as a makeshift piano stool and beckoning me to sit down on it.

I raised the lid and began to play a Scarlatti sonatina that would cover a wide range of keys, the kind of piece of a piano tuner might play to test his work at the end of a job.

'Lovely,' I declared, sitting back to admire the brass candlesticks either side of the music stand as I wondered what to play next.

'I'm so glad you like it. I was a bit worried when I saw Laurel and Hardy there trying to shift it up the stairs, but I've checked the casing all over and by some miracle it's unscathed.'

'It's lovely,' I repeated. 'It has a surprisingly rich tone for an upright, and the movement of the keys is like silk. Where has it come from?'

'I texted my mum and dad in Clevedon the morning after I'd heard you play your parents' baby grand to ask if I could have their old upright. Neither Mum nor Dad play, and their piano's just been gathering dust since Horace and I stopped having lessons when we were kids. They've been saying for ages they wanted to get rid of it to free up some space in their lounge, so when I asked, they arranged to get it delivered here straight away.'

'So are you thinking of taking up lessons again?'

'Oh no, sweetheart, this isn't for me to play, it's for you. While we were away, I realised you need a piano like your mum needs the open water, and your dad needs his Munros.'

'And what about you?' I asked, getting up from the stool and turning to place my arms around Hector's neck. 'What do you need?'

He put his head on one side.

'Oh, I've got everything I need, thank you very much.' He kissed me lightly on the lips before drawing me closer to him. 'You see, Sophie Sayers, I've got you.'

ACKNOWLEDGMENTS

First of all, I am forever indebted to my Scottish husband Gordon for introducing me to the delights of Scotland, and to his addiction to Munro-bagging that has enabled me to see more of Scotland than a lot of Scottish nationals (yes, he's bagged them all). This story is partly born out of my love of Scotland, of the Highlands, and of their capital city, Inverness. If you've never been there, I hope it will encourage you to visit.

For the sake of fun, I have created fictitious tourist attractions that those with local knowledge may guess were inspired by the wonderful Highland Folk Museum in Newtonmore; Leakey's iconic second-hand bookshop; the multi-featured corporation sports complex Inverness Leisure; and the Jacobite Cruise company that offers boat trips from Inverness to Castle Urquhart. I've fictionalised them to make it clear that the real destinations are all very safe places to visit! I Should Cocoa was inspired by the completely addictive SoCoCo on Inverness High Street, and I'm sad to have learned that since my last visit it has ceased trading. Gretna Green, Dalwhinnie, the Inverness City Museum, Whin Park, the Old High Church, Castle Urquhart, and Loch Ness are entirely real. As to the Loch Ness Monster, if you can't decide, a trip to the Loch Ness Centre and Exhibition will give you a fine array of stories that you may or may not wish to believe.

Thanks to Shaun Bythell of The Bookshop in Wigtown, Scotland's National Book Town, for his bestselling series of memoirs, of which *The Diary of a Bookseller* is the first. He has taught me so much about the second-hand book trade from the bookseller's perspective. Alasdair Graham is not based on Shaun Bythell in any way.

Thanks also to Calum MacLean and his excellent book, *1001 Outdoor Swimming Tips*, for helping me learn more about the appeal and perils of that hobby without having to get wet myself, and to Orna Ross and Tara Loder, both enthusiastic swimmers, for their input, and for clarifying that as Orna patiently told me, 'When I was growing up, we just called it swimming.'

I'm grateful to Fiona Dishington, volunteer tour guide at the Old High Church, for telling me about its graveyard's extraordinary history.

As ever, I am very grateful to Team Boldwood, led by the amazing Amanda Ridout, for turning my manuscript into a book in so many different formats – to my editor Tara Loder, copy-editor Sandra Ferguson, Susan Lamprell, proofreader Emily Reader (what a great example of nominative determinism!), marketing team Nia Beynon, Claire Fenby, Jenna Houston, Marcela Torres, and Ben Wilson; to my agent Ethan Ellenberg for his constant guidance and encouragement; and to Lorna Fergusson of Fictionfire.com for being my Scottish sensitivity reader. Any remaining errors are my own.

On the home front, huge thanks to my daughter Laura for her practical help and moral support as my office assistant. I can't wait to visit Inverness again with Gordon and Laura.

MORE FROM DEBBIE YOUNG

We hope you enjoyed reading *Murder in the Highlands*. If you did, please leave a review.

If you'd like to gift a copy, this book is also available as an ebook, hardback, large print, digital audio download and audiobook CD.

Sign up to Debbie Youngs' mailing list for news, competitions and updates on future books.

https://bit.ly/DebbieYoungNews

Why not explore the rest of the Sophie Sayers Cozy Mystery series...

ABOUT THE AUTHOR

Debbie Young is the much-loved author of the Sophie Sayers and St Bride's cozy crime mysteries. She lives in a Cotswold village, where she runs the local literary festival, and has worked at Westonbirt School, both of which provide inspiration for her writing.

Visit Debbie's Website: www.authordebbieyoung.com

facebook.com/AuthorDebbieYoung

instagram.com/debbieyoungauthor

twitter.com/DebbieYoungBN

bookbub.com/authors/debbie-young

youtube.com/youngbyname

Poison & Pens

POISON & PENS IS THE HOME OF
COZY MYSTERIES SO POUR YOURSELF
A CUP OF TEA & GET SLEUTHING!

DISCOVER PAGE-TURNING NOVELS FROM
YOUR FAVOURITE AUTHORS &
MEET NEW FRIENDS

Boldwood

Boldwood Books is an award-winning fiction publishing company seeking out the best stories from around the world.

Find out more at www.boldwoodbooks.com

Join our reader community for brilliant books, competitions and offers!

Follow us
@BoldwoodBooks
@BookandTonic

Sign up to our weekly deals newsletter

https://bit.ly/BoldwoodBNewsletter